MW00652277

What New Beg........gs ... iviauc ...

New beginnings take courage…

She's a fifty-five-year-old widow feeling like she's lost herself.

On a whim of her aching heart, Alice McIntyre buys the Star Gazer Inn and is looking for a fresh start…something to put a spark back into her life.

But first she has to tell her four sons, who have problems of their own but have smothered her with their protective instincts. She's lived on the huge South Texas ranch just outside of Corpus Christi since their father carried her over the threshold. She's raised them on the massive McIntyre Ranch—one of the largest, wealthiest in Texas. It's been her home and theirs. Will they understand that it's time for her to leave? Time for her to move on?

Jackson McIntyre is shocked by his mother's announcement. Guilt-ridden in the aftermath of his father's accident, Jackson is determined to do whatever it takes to help his mother find her way to move forward. But this new idea of hers has him reeling.

Nina lives next door to the inn and is living a quiet life,

keeping a low profile. She has her reasons. Will the opening of the inn and her new neighbors, especially the oldest son of the new innkeeper, tempt her to step back into the light and out of the shadows of her past?

Lisa, Alice's best friend and recent divorcee, has been traveling the world since the breakup that left her shaken and feeling just as lost as Alice. A brilliant cook with a flair for entertaining, she loves Alice's idea and joins her to open the inn. But Lisa has her own secrets.

Can these two friends, and their new neighbor Nina, find fresh starts as they ready the Star Gazer Inn for its new beginning?

Will Nina find the courage to take one more chance on love with her new friend's son?

Three women find friendship and courage on the shores of Corpus Christi Bay. Come visit the Star Gazer Inn, with a side trip to the McIntyre Ranch, as Alice finds her way between two worlds.

This new series follows Alice, her sons, and her friends—and new loves—on the South Texas coast with its sparkling topaz water.

You'll want to dip your toes in and stay awhile.

WHAT NEW BEGINNINGS ARE MADE OF

Star Gazer Inn of Corpus Christi Bay, Book One

DEBRA CLOPTON

What New Beginnings are Made of

Copyright © 2020 Debra Clopton Parks

This book is a work of fiction. Names and characters are of the author's imagination or are used fictitiously. Any resemblance to an actual person, living or dead, is entirely coincidental.

All rights reserved. No part of this publication may be reproduced, distributed or transmitted in any form or by any means, including photocopying, recording, or other electronic or mechanical methods, without the prior written permission of the publisher, except in the case of brief quotations embodied in critical reviews and certain other noncommercial uses permitted by copyright law. For permission requests, the author through her website: www.debraclopton.com

CHAPTER ONE

Alice McIntyre stood on the sun-drenched beach of Star Gazer Island and breathed deeply of the salty air and dug her toes into the soft sugar sand. The scents and feels grounded her and, for the moment, staved off the loneliness that clung to her.

"I miss you, William," she whispered into the wind as she wrapped her arms around herself and fought off the threatening tears. It had been fifteen months since her husband's tragic death, and grief still came to hit her hard at unexpected moments, leaving her speechless and crying and missing him so much it hurt.

The soothing sound of the incoming waves washed through her muddled thoughts. Days like this, she left the ranch and came here to this beautiful beach, where she'd met her William and where she still felt closer to him.

She tried hard not to worry her sons. Even though they were grown men, she didn't want them worrying about her. And they would, thinking she was theirs to protect and coddle. They had done that well—too well, almost. She felt smothered sometimes. So, on the pretext of going to lunch with friends, she would often drive here to Star Gazer Island, overlooking the bay of Corpus Christi, and she walked along the shoreline with her memories. Or sat in the sand, with her arms wrapped around her knees, and listened to the water and watched the waves as the tide washed in and washed out. The sea had a peace to it that calmed her and dulled the heavy burden of loss that would overtake her.

She was a strong woman, always had been. To be married to William McIntyre, one had to be strong. Her husband had a dynamic, sometimes overbearing personality but was always kind, entertaining and so much larger than life than anyone she had ever known. Everyone loved him but she had loved him with all of her heart. And her love story began here.

She turned from the ocean to peer toward the old inn. Back then, thirty-five years ago, when she'd been working at the Star Gazer Inn during her first year of college, the place was a thriving destination for vacationers. They'd flock to the quaint ten-bedroom inn, with its award-winning cuisine served on the beautiful veranda overlooking the fabulous blue waters by day and at night the sparkling moonlight on the water and the lights of Corpus Christi across the bay. It had been an enchanting place.

That inn had closed about five years ago, and for some unfathomable reason, no one had reopened it. It hurt Alice's heart to see it sitting there abandoned when she felt such a strong, happy connection to it.

Now it sat there with its pale-gray paint, looking forlorn and lost—a mirror of how Alice felt, she realized suddenly. The inn sat on a generous section of land with an overgrown flower garden and an open area where there used to be a gazebo and she remembered them errecting a large tent when someone booked a wedding.

She'd met William when he had come for a vacation with his family. From the moment she'd offered him a menu that first night when he'd sat down on the veranda for dinner, there had been an instant connection. He had sought her out all weekend. One thing about William was that when he saw something he liked, he went after it with single-minded determination. And he'd liked her very much. They were ranchers. Very wealthy ranchers, she'd learned from one of the other waitresses. They owned a ranch just thirty minutes away from Star Gazer Island, and by the end of the weekend, he and his family had invited her out to the McIntyre Ranch.

From the moment she saw the ranch, she'd loved it. Just like she'd known instantly that she loved William. What was not to love? He was an amazing man. He'd been as rugged as the South Texas ranch, and very soon they were married, and he had carried her over the threshold of his home on the ranch, one of the largest in Texas. It had been mind-blowing to a young woman who had grown up in a home of modest means.

Through the years, she would come back to the inn with friends, when the house full of men she'd given birth to overwhelmed her, and enjoy some girl time. They would go to other places too, but this had always been her favorite place.

Standing there now, looking at the big inn with its once bright-yellow Adirondack chairs, now faded with time, the crazy thought that had tugged at her for months sparked. A flickering flame suddenly caught and burned bright in her mind.

A whisper of hope, of purpose, filled her.

Compelled by a force other than her own will, Alice crossed the sand. It squished between her toes and the warmth of it at this hour of day wasn't so hot that she couldn't stand walking across it barefooted. At the weathered picket fence, she dropped her flip-flops on the path and slipped into them, then walked into the garden that stood between the inn and the water. She stared at the inn. Up closer, it didn't look as if it had weathered the years too terribly bad. It even looked as if someone had done some work on it. Curious now, she walked around the side of the inn, certain since she was last here that someone had cleaned up the place. She walked through the side gate onto the concrete drive and walked to the road. There, sticking out of the grass, was a fresh new For Sale sign.

Walking over, she laid her hand on the wooden sign and studied it, almost not believing that maybe after all these years the owners had taken an interest in selling it again. She turned and looked at the house, a combination of Victorian era and welcoming beach house. With its enormous windows and wide porches, it was beautiful. Next door to it sat a cute red cottage with white trim, and from the sandy beach, she had also seen the yellow Adirondack chairs sitting on its porch. It was an adorable, cozy place, and when the inn had been a thriving place, it had been the owner's cottage and was obviously still lived in and loved by someone.

On a whim, Alice used her phone to take a picture of the For Sale sign. And then, not exactly sure what she was thinking or contemplating, she walked back around through the backyard and out to the sand again. A buzz of excitement hummed through her as Alice walked down the beach, her thoughts no longer on her suffocating grief but on something new...something that had taken hold, like sunshine breaking through the clouds after a storm.

She looked back over her shoulder at the Star Gazer Inn and she smiled.

* * *

One month later

Jackson McIntyre's mother had just dropped a bombshell on him.

"Could you say that again?" He stared at his mother, who stood near the window of the oversized office of the McIntyre Ranch. He was certain he'd heard her correctly, but he needed her to confirm the declaration because it was so out of character for her.

The McIntyre Ranch wasn't the size of the King Ranch, but the two hundred thousand acres of South Texas land their ranch spread across made them one of the largest cattle ranches in the Lone Star State. With their cattle business, their quarter horse breeding program and the oil that ran beneath the grazing land,

Jackson and his three brothers were very wealthy men. Their mother was too. She didn't need to do this. That was what was so baffling.

Upon the death of their father, the larger-than-life William McIntyre II, they could have hired a ranch manager and never worked another day in their lives if they hadn't wanted to work—however, they wanted to work. But their mother? No way she needed to.

Like their grandfathers before them and their father too, Jackson, Riley, Tucker, and Dallas thrived on working the ranch and continuing the legacy of the McIntyres. They'd learned to ride almost before they could walk in a straight line and were involved in cattle roundups before they'd lost their baby teeth. Since their great-great-grandfather had been a steamship captain in the 1800's and they'd grown up on hearing stories of his adventures, a deep love of both the land and the water was in the brothers' blood. And their mother's too, it seemed.

Sitting behind the huge walnut desk that had been his grandfather's, then his father's and was now his, at thirty-five years of age, Jackson felt the weight of the responsibility heavy on his shoulders as he studied his mother.

Alice McIntyre, as always, was perfectly put together in her stylish jeans, white linen blouse, and black slide sandals. She believed in elegance but comfort, in both her clothing and her lifestyle. Staring back at him, she tilted her head to the side, and her blue eyes softened, as if understanding this was hard for him to digest.

This bombshell had come out of nowhere.

She took a deep breath and pushed her jaw-length blonde hair behind an ear as Jackson waited for her to speak. He loved his mother very much and had been concerned for her ever since the death of his father. Jackson ignored the knife slashing through his own heart at the very thought of that day. This was about his mother, not him, and the hole in his own heart. And the guilt that clung to him like quicksand, sucking him in at times. That guilt was all the more reason he had vowed beyond anything that he would take care of his mother in the absence of his father.

"I know it's a shock, Jackson, but you heard me correctly. I've bought a quaint, adorable little inn on Star Gazer Island. It's the inn I worked at in college and where I met your father. I plan to freshen it up and open it back up. I'll be moving in and running it—"

He'd heard her right. "But Mom, your life is here on the ranch. You can't just pack up and leave. You have everything you need here; working is certainly not something you need to do."

Her eyes flashed, and she lifted her chin stubbornly, as she was known to do. "And why not?

You and I both know that you boys don't need me here anymore. And, to be quite frank, I've lived here since I was nineteen years old and your father and I got married. I've lived in this house since William carried me over that threshold. That's a long time. And as much as it grieves me, your father isn't here any longer, and you boys aren't children anymore. And, may I remind you, there are no grandkids here to hold me. I gave birth to you a little over a year after I moved into this home and I've loved every moment of it. I've happily been a wife, mother and one day hopefully a grandmother but I've decided I can't wait around for that any longer. I don't want to just sit here twiddling my thumbs and watching the flowers in my garden grow. I'm only fifty-five, and I want something different now. I need something more than my gardening and watching you boys work the ranch."

Her words hit hard, causing more guilt to slice through him. He was the oldest and probably should have married by now. His mother had no grandchildren, and that, too, was his fault. He stood and moved from behind the desk. He measured his words. "Mom, we need you. We...this place won't be the same without you."

His heart squeezed at the thought of no longer having his father here on the ranch, but not having his mother here too was a startling blow. He realized that it was a selfish thought on his part.

She walked over to him and placed her small hand on his heart as she looked up at him. His small mother, with her fine-featured face and her sapphire eyes that were such a contrast from the brown-toned eyes and chiseled features that he and his brothers had inherited from their father. Everything about her seemed softer than anything out here on the ranch. She softened the edges of this rugged land that surrounded the ranch.

"Son, you're the head of this family now. And one day I hope you're going to finally marry. Then your wife will be the woman of this house, and of this ranch. I've been that for most of my life and, to be honest, at this time, well...I need something more. And I've already bought the inn. Burt helped me—don't get mad at him," she added quickly, holding her hand up when he would have said something. "He did it under duress. I had to twist his arm, basically, to get it done, but he did it out of respect for your father and for me."

Jackson would have a word with Burt. Burt Dobbs was a lawyer and also Jackson's father's best friend. Burt's law firm handled all of McIntyre Enterprises' legal matters and he had done this without a word to him. But then again, that didn't surprise Jackson because Burt's loyalty would lie with his mother and his father. At least Jackson knew that if Burt was involved, things had been done correctly. "He should have said something to me."

"No, he shouldn't have. Now, I'm moving in three days. I just wanted you to hear it from me before you heard it from anyone else. I'll tell your brothers at dinner tonight."

Feeling the strain, he turned and looked out the same window his mother had been looking out of and at the great view of her gardens, meticulously maintained, mostly by her own hands. She worked tirelessly in those gardens and here in this dry country, growing flowers—other than the varieties that took the heat well—wasn't the easiest feat to do. But Alice had a green thumb, and she coaxed them to life and maintained them by spending hours out there tending to them.

Maybe she did need something different in her life. He personally couldn't imagine spending all that time digging in the dirt. Now, he loved cattle—loved everything about the oil business and everything about the cattle and the horse industry. But planting and watering flowers—not so much.

His mother had seemed lost since losing her life partner. Maybe she did need a change, and he'd vowed to do everything in his power to help her get through this.

"All right, then, I guess I understand." At least he would try to understand and support her. "What do I need to do to help you? You tell me and I'll make it happen."

He knew that's what his dad would expect of him. And at this point, after living life without him, they all still grieved, all still couldn't believe he was gone.

He and his brothers dealt with their grief through working the land and the cattle William had loved so much. They worked harder than before, each seeking to find their way forward without their dad as they continued the legacy founded by their grandfather and broadened by their father. The idea of doing it without his mom here didn't sit well, but if that was what she wanted, then he'd move heaven and earth to help her get what she needed to move forward. Because, in a similar way, he was floundering also. He'd lost the greatest man Jackson had ever known, and he was still struggling. But life must go on. And it seemed life changed as well.

"Thank you, Jackson. We will continue to put one foot in front of the other like we've been doing. I've just added a plot twist. You can help me move."

It was a plot twist, all right. He just prayed it was the right twist for her.

CHAPTER TWO

Nina Hanson pulled the animal carrier out of the back seat of her Mini Cooper convertible and set it on the ground. Her heart beat quickly as she crouched down, opened the latch and let the fuzzy golden-haired pup free. She was beautiful, about three months old and full of boundless energy.

"Welcome to your new home, Buttercup. I'm so glad to have you here." Nina smiled happily as the new addition to her family sprang from the carrier and jumped up, putting her paws on Nina's leg as it danced an excited jig, wiggling from head to toe.

She'd been debating on a puppy for a while now and had finally gone down to the shelter. Buttercup, the cutest curly-haired Goldendoodle had won her heart instantly.

It wasn't the same as bringing home a baby, but it was as close as Nina would get at this point and time in her life. She longed for a baby but after her luck with relationships, a baby seemed impossible—unless she adopted on her own, and Nina wasn't ready to make that commitment just yet. Not while her life was in flux because of her last dating disaster.

Not wanting to ruin this perfect moment, she scooped Buttercup into her hands and held her up so she could look into her sweet eyes. "I've had terrible luck with men, little one. But you and I will be fine. Who needs men anyway?" she asked, with a matter-of-fact nod of her head. She was making it on her own and she would just keep it that way.

Her and Buttercup against the world.

Shoving the nudge of loneliness away, she cuddled the wiggly pup as she stood. Then, leaving the carrier on the grass, she walked to her cottage, mounted the three steps and sank into one of the bright-yellow Adirondack chairs with the colorful pillows. From here, she could look out across the street to the dunes that blocked most of her view from this vantage point. But the dunes were wild and rugged-looking, and she loved looking at them. She loved painting them. However, it was her view from the back porch that had her renting the property. It was a spectacular view across the bay of sparkling topaz ocean, with only a white sandy stretch of beach between her back porch and the water. She loved walking on the beach early in the morning and then drinking coffee on her deck before she started working on the art project of the day.

The seclusion her little red cottage had here on the end of this barrier island was perfect for her in so many ways—for her work and for her need to keep a low profile. She had noticed that the For Sale sign on the vacant inn next door had disappeared recently and was curious whether it had sold. If it had sold, then she would lose some privacy but surely after all this time, she didn't have to worry.

Cuddling Buttercup close, she ran her hand along the pup's curly golden fur and started to get up and head to the backyard but she paused as a car passed by on the quiet road. It would turn around at the dead end and then drive back by when it realized there was no place to park the car for beach access this far down.

The puppy wiggled, reminding her she had been taking it to the backyard so it could be safe from the road. Suddenly Buttercup sprang from her arms and raced down the steps.

"Wait!" Nina hurried after the pup. Frantic, she watched it race across her yard and run like a flash across the old inn's yard and disappear around the corner of the quaint inn.

She rounded the corner of the front porch and halted at the sight of a four-door black pickup truck in the driveway. Feeling all the more driven to catch her puppy, she hurried past the truck, calling out for Buttercup to stop. But the puppy ignored her as it scampered through the opened wooden gate into the backyard of the inn.

"Please don't get into anything," she muttered as she followed it through the gate and ran straight into the solid wall of a hard chest.

Shocked and embarrassed, she bounced back and looked into brown eyes, chocolate mocha with a hint of gold undertones that glinted despite the shadow of the black Stetson on the handsome man's head. Neatly cut dark hair peeked from beneath the hat, complementing sun-bronzed skin that spoke of the South Texas area and time outdoors.

Involuntarily, she trembled.

"Whoa there. Are you okay?"

"Fine," she managed, struggling to catch her breath, to not panic. The guy was handsome and non-threatening, she reminded herself firmly before she made a fool of herself. He held Buttercup under one arm and looked at her with concern.

"I-I was just chasing this little rascal. Thankfully, I see you've caught her."

WHAT NEW BEGINNINGS ARE MADE OF

The cowboy took a second before he pulled his gaze off her face, as if sensing her turmoil, before looking down at her wiggling puppy. He held Buttercup up to his face and stared into the pups deep-blue eyes as a warm, sexy smile spread across his face.

A startling eruption of frantic butterflies swarmed in Nina's chest at the sight of that smile. Her reaction to this man was as intense as his eyes.

And hard to ignore. She attempted it anyway.

He tucked Buttercup against his chest and focused his gaze back on her. She tried to hide the melding of mixed emotions rioting through her.

"I heard you call her name and was coming to investigate when she came bounding around the house and ran into my feet. I grabbed her up, hoping she hadn't hurt herself and because that road is fairly busy this morning with people driving to the turn-around looking at the water."

Whether he meant the comment as a prod for reckless endangerment of her puppy or not, she took it that way. "She got away from me for only a moment. I'm very aware of the road, and honestly, its not as if it's Main Street or something." She felt bad about saying that because it only took one car to hit Buttercup and cause her harm. Still, irritation at his comment had her hackles rising. Plus, he was…well, so very attractive and she was noticing him, something

17

she really didn't want to do.

"No offense meant."

His calm words made her words seem more defensive than necessary. However, the way her pulse continued to race, she couldn't help it. She'd believed herself to be immune to dark-headed men with interest in their eyes. And she wasn't happy that this man had breached the barriers she'd erected with a single smile.

She lifted her chin as much in defiance of her own reaction to the man than anything he'd said. "I adopted Buttercup an hour ago at the shelter. My nerves are a little rattled at how quickly she escaped my arms and ran over here." Her nerves were rattled more now looking at this man and feeling as if she had to justify herself to him. "She scrambled free and raced over here. But I can assure you it wasn't on purpose," she ground out the last sentence, frustrated with him and herself for rattling on and on.

"I'm glad you rescued her. I'm used to a ranch where a dog can run and play and work to its heart's content, with no boundaries. Having to worry about getting run over by cars is a highly improbable situation. So I'm sorry if I sounded unfeeling."

She relaxed at his calm apology but was unsure how to answer him.

"I'll need to make sure my mom understands that if she decides to get a pet," he continued stroking

Buttercup's golden fur as she rested against his chest. It was an act of comfort and Buttercup relished it by the look on her little doggy face.

Nina focused on his words and not how lucky the puppy was at the moment. "Your mother—is she going to be my neighbor? Or you?"

"My mother bought the inn, and I just learned of her purchase yesterday. She'll be moving in later this week. I'm checking it out and the neighborhood. She told me it needed some work. And from the look of the outside, she's right. But it's nothing major."

She relaxed, knowing he was the son of her soon-to-be new neighbor and that he was not her new neighbor. "It's been empty the entire three years that I've been here." *Why had she told him how long she'd lived here?*

"You've lived in this neighborhood for three years? How is it?"

She stiffened, not in the habit of giving out details of her life these days, but the damage was already done. "It's quiet for the most part down on this end of the peninsula but in the summer months the beach can be busy. The town itself is low-keyed, and safe."

"Good to know. My mother has lived on our family ranch for most of her adult life, since she married my late father. This will be new for her, and for me worrying about her."

His father was dead, and his mother was moving here off the family ranch and it worried him. That was a lot of information and as she looked at him, she understood he felt responsible for his mother.

"I've never had any trouble from anyone here. If that helps ease your mind."

"It does. I'm sure you and my mother will get along well. And by the way, she loves animals, so you don't have to worry about her not wanting your puppy around."

"That's good to know."

He handed Buttercup back to her and their hands brushed as they made the tradeoff. She did not like the tingle of awareness that radiated through her arm and then through her entire body, but to her surprise, she didn't jump away from the contact.

"Thank you. It looks like you're a dog lover too." *Why did she say that?*

"I have two dogs. Cattle dogs. They're good workers."

"And that's what makes a good dog, that it be a good worker?" Irritation pricked as much from his remark as at herself for letting her guard down with him.

"On a ranch, a cattle dog earns its keep. My dogs can bring a herd in by themselves if I need them to. And they do it a lot. They're very good workers;

otherwise they're useless."

She frowned at him. "Then I guess you'd say Buttercup is useless. She won't be earning her keep. She'll be my companion. And loved by me simply for her sweetness and willingness to love me back." It was time to call this conversation over. "Thank you for catching her for me, and I look forward to meeting your mother."

More than ready for some distance, she turned to go, with Buttercup squirming until she could look over Nina's shoulder at the cowboy. And to Nina's annoyance, before she rounded the corner, she also looked back over her shoulder.

He was watching her and tipped his hat at her.

Only then did it dawn on her that she hadn't gotten his name and he hadn't offered it.

And that was just fine. She hadn't offered her name either.

CHAPTER THREE

On the drive over the bridge, back toward the ranch, Jackson had his windows rolled down, to keep the scent of the ocean with him as long as he could before the dusty heated air of the ranch replaced it. He loved the ranch, but the ocean had its perks, too, and the scent and the beauty could not be denied. He studied the sparkling blue waters of Corpus Christi Bay. He was always amazed at the beauty of it, always glad that he lived between the two worlds of beaches, sunsets, and soft white sand and the ranch with its scrub brush, cactus, cattle, and horses.

He got why his mother needed a change. The ranch land could be harsh, especially in mid-summer, and she was a good drive away from everything. The city by the bay had a beauty that he enjoyed, and Star Gazer Island was small and, from what the new neighbor had said, safe. He felt better about his mom being in the smaller subsection rather than the city. Most of all, he hoped that at the inn she found what she was looking for.

That she found the healing to her heart that he knew she still needed.

He had to make a few changes there himself after looking at it; he wanted to make sure she had the best protection, with alarm systems and everything else she needed to be safe. He had made a few calls and found a respected contractor to come look and to meet his mother. She'd have to make the call on who did the work. He'd just made the initial call at her request. She understood his need to make sure she was safe, considering she would be living at the inn with strangers.

Burt had also received a call from him, and he'd let the lawyer know he wasn't happy not to have been brought in on the idea before it had gone to the buying stage. Burt had understood his anger but had pointed out that when Alice got her mind set on something, nobody talked her out of it. She'd also threatened his life if he revealed her secret before she did it.

His mother had known Jackson would have tried to stop her if he had known earlier.

His hands tightened on the steering wheel as

tension knotted between his shoulder blades. She would be okay. Why did he feel like a parent whose kid was going off to college or something? This was his mother; she was a grown woman who was plenty capable of taking care of herself. Maybe he'd been holding her back with all of his worrying over her.

His brothers had told him he was turning old before his time and needed to chill out. Maybe they'd been right. He forced his grip to ease up, then removed his left hand and hung it out the window like he used to do when he was a kid, riding in the truck with his dad. He let the air filter through his fingers, letting the tension in his shoulders ease as he remembered happier times.

He missed his dad. But they were all learning to live with it. *Deal with it was a better term.* Pushing that thought aside, he concentrated on the wind sifting through his fingers.

Burt had said they all needed to do whatever they had to in order to help his mother get through the grieving process of losing the great love of her life. That was code for letting her go.

Jackson would make sure she was safe, and he'd check on her too much, but she was going to have to deal with that until he knew for certain she was safe. *If he was going to let her do this...* He said that lightly because his mother was small, but she'd give him an earful if she got even a hint of thoughts like that. She

24

might have lived on the ranch all these years and let his father have his way most of the time—but the keywords were "let him," because when she really wanted something, she got it. Even if that meant putting her size-six foot down hard until anyone standing in her way relented.

Including his dad.

She was a force to be reckoned with when she set her mind on something; she didn't stop until she got it. That person whom they all loved dearly had become a shadow, seeming to have lost herself. She spent most of her time puttering in the gardens with her flowers. Her doing this on her own, buying this inn, was a glimpse of his spirited mother. Maybe this venture would help her find whatever it was she was looking for.

He liked that she had a neighbor. There were a few houses on the street but not many, so he was glad that the lady next door seemed nice, and responsible. He hadn't gotten her name, but he would. She could be a great asset to have next door if his mother ran into any trouble.

And, the neighbor with no name had been pretty. Not in your classic over-the-top pretty but in a wholesome way that pulled on his protective instincts. Why, he wasn't sure. But it was true, and as he drove up the drive of the ranch and parked near the horse barn, he anticipated seeing her again.

As he climbed out of the truck, he saw Shep and Socks come running, tails wagging. Tucker and Riley came out of the stable behind them and also headed his way. By the looks on their faces, they had something big on their minds. Their mother, most likely.

"Hey, pups." He stopped to rub both dogs behind the ears. "I'm glad y'all look happier to see me than those two." The dogs wiggled from head to toe, and he laughed at their excitement. Immediately, he thought of his mom's neighbor and her jab that she loved her dog even though it wasn't earning its keep. "You two earn your keep. And then some."

He straightened as his brothers reached him. He knew exactly why they looked so fierce. "So you talked to Mom?"

"I don't like it." Riley crossed his arms and gave Jackson a do-you-hear-me glare.

The youngest of the family, Riley tended to not like surprises unless he was the one doing the surprising.

"I don't either." Tucker crossed his arms and frowned.

"Calm down. I know you don't like it, and I don't either. But what we like isn't relevant. Mom has bought herself an inn on Star Gazer Island. Whether we want it or not, she's moving out tomorrow and into her new home."

"And you're just now telling us?" Tucker's

expression was fierce.

"So, she just did this all on her own is what you're saying? She went out and found this place and bought it, and she just said she needs to do it because she needs to do it."

"That about sums it up correctly, Tuck. I went over there, checked the place out this morning. It's weary-looking but Mom will have it looking great quickly, I'm sure. You know how she can get things done when she sets her mind to it. And just so you all know, I told Burt he should have let us know what was going on but he informed me that his loyalty lies with Mom right now, that Dad would have wanted him to do what she wanted. He assured me that he checked it out to make sure it was a good deal and if it hadn't been, he would have talked her out of it or let us know. But he also reminded me that she would have bought it anyway if it was what she really wanted. And the reality is that's the truth. So I just got back from checking it out. Like I said, it needs some sprucing up but as far as I can tell, structurally, it's good. There was an inspection with the purchase and it said it was structurally sound. So we have to take the professionals' word on that. As for renovations, that's up to her what she wants but I'm planning on helping her in any way I can."

"I will too," Riley said. "If she wants it, then she should have it."

"I agree," Tucker said, though sounding less than enthusiastic.

"Her neighbor seems nice." Jackson thought of the pretty neighbor. "A woman with a puppy who says it's safe. I think she'll make a good neighbor for Mom."

"Good to know," Tucker said. "Is she Mom's age?"

"Younger. Probably in her thirties."

"That'll work," Riley said. "Maybe we can persuade her to call us if she sees anything off at the inn—you know, lurkers or unruly types."

"Maybe. But I'm having a top-of-the-line security system installed. That will help us sleep better at night. But y'all, something Burt said hit me. He said that we need to support Mom in doing whatever she needs to do in order to move on. So that's what I'm going to do. Moving van gets here early in the morning, and she's taking what she wants. I told her whatever—it's her stuff. She says she's not taking much, that the inn will have a different look than the ranch."

"She'll probably make it fluffy." Riley grinned.

Tucker looked skeptical. "What does that mean?"

"You know, girly. Like pink couches and white chairs. There probably won't be a lick of leather in the place. Women like things that look like you need to be wearing a suit to fit in. At least that's the impression I get when I pick up my dates at their apartments. If I went by after getting finished working cattle, they wouldn't have let me in the door."

Working cattle was a dusty, sweaty business. "I'm guessing that's why your dating life is a revolving door?"

Riley shrugged. "That's part of it. I'm looking for 'the one,' you know, and she will have to take me in all forms. Including the dusty form who loves the cattle business. Like Mom did Dad. Anyway, I'll do what I can to help Mom move on. I've got a crew out on the west side working cattle. We're moving to the coast later this week, and I need to check on them. Talk to y'all later."

Tucker shifted. "Jack, I want what's best for Mom, so I'll do what I need to do to help." He started toward the barn. "But right now, I need to ride some colts. Sale is coming and they need more saddle time."

Jackson watched his brothers leave. He had more paperwork to do, which seemed to be more and more his lot in life since his dad died. He needed more saddle time and decided then and there to start getting back outside more, dealing with the part of ranching he loved. But he also had to help his mother.

It bothered him some that she seemed set on not taking much from the house, not taking things that reminded her of her life here. That bothered him because she might be trying to forget her life here on the ranch with all of them. He didn't voice that concern, knowing in his heart it was unfair. The inn

29

DEBRA CLOPTON

would be on the coast and of course require a different look, a lighter feeling…more carefree. And that was probably what his mother was seeking in her own life.

He'd felt it today when he'd been on Star Gazer Island. Even for himself, it had been a refreshing feeling.

Truth was, he was in a rut and he needed to dig himself out, which was what his mother was doing.

He needed to take notes.

* * *

Alice stood on the back porch of the inn. The moving van would be here tomorrow with the few things that she was bringing with her to the inn, but she'd wanted to drop by today and make a to-do list. And just because she couldn't help herself. Excitement bubbled inside her.

Looking out over the overgrown backyard separating her from the expanse of white sand leading out to the gorgeous topaz water, she breathed in the scent of honeysuckle growing on the arch, mingled with the scents of salt and clean, fresh ocean air. Her heart swelled at being here. At knowing she owned the inn and was about to begin a new chapter in her life.

She had done it.

Taken the steps she needed to, and now the inevitable changes in her life spread out before her,

30

both challenging and welcomed.

A part of her hurt terribly at what she was leaving behind. A part of her that wanted to turn around and race back to her home on the ranch with all of her beloved boys, the memories of her life there with William and the charmed life she'd lived with him there. The photos scattered throughout the house, reminding her of all she'd had and what she'd lost…

She closed her eyes as a wave of regret came over her so strong it threatened to bring a tidal wave of tears to consume her and drop her to her knees. She'd cried a river in the gardens of the house since losing William. She hadn't needed to water the plants; her tears seemed enough to do it. She wasn't expecting to not cry here, but at least there was newness here and the spark of hope she hadn't felt in a while. The spark of still more living to come in her life. Not that the fullness of it had come and gone with William. Oh, how she missed him. But she had to step over the line of what was and move into the light of today…and tomorrow and onward.

And here she would move on without feeling guilty about the change she was making. All of her life she'd been needed, felt she had a purpose as William's wife and of being her sons' mother. But her sons were busy and were not children anymore. And she was at loose ends. Restless. It was time for a change.

Thankfully, her sweet boys—men now, so much

like their father—were supporting her in this. Dallas, who was on the rodeo circuit and unable to get home, had told her to do what she had to do when she'd called him yesterday after talking with Jackson. Riley and Tucker had given her their support this morning after their initial shock last night when she'd told them what she'd done. She knew they'd come out and do whatever she needed them to do. Jackson had been a rock of support after his own shocked reaction. He'd come out this morning before she'd driven over and he'd checked things out. Their father would be proud of his boys. She was proud of them too for their understanding, even if it was with some reluctance on their parts. She would have hated to tell them with or without their support she was going through with her plans. But they'd chosen to support her in what she wanted. What she needed.

William had always known she wanted a beach house and had promised they would buy one. Or build one on the coastal land the ranch owned. But time had slipped away and the beach house hadn't become a reality. She loved the beach, loved this view looking at the water, and now she had it. Time wasn't slipping away from her anymore. Time was of the essence…William's death had taught her that.

A knot tightened in her chest. In some ways, she was being rebellious. Tears stung her eyes at the thought. She had loved her husband very much, but her need for something more than the ranch hadn't been a priority. The ranch, the cattle, the business had always come first. But now, taking her future into her own hands, here she was. So why was it that doing this and then the thoughts she sometimes had made her feel as if she were doing something she shouldn't do?

Shaking off those suddenly pressing thoughts, she reached for her yellow sun hat and light canvas bag and headed down the walk on the side of the inn and down the drive. When she reached the front yard, she looked up at the cotton candy clouds dotting the blue sky. A perfect day to walk the scant distance to town. She had things to buy, and shopping locally was where she wanted to start. Her things would arrive tomorrow. Tomorrow it would be official and her work would begin.

Her steps were as light as the clouds above as Alice walked toward town, smiling.

CHAPTER FOUR

Nina was on her back porch, setting up her paints
when she heard a noise coming from next door. It
was a beeping noise. Realizing that the cowboy from a
few days ago said that his mother would be moving in
soon, she set her paintbrush in the turpentine, then
walked off the porch and passed her hydrangeas to the
wooden gate that opened into her side yard between
her house and the inn. Buttercup was asleep in the
corner of the kitchen so Nina didn't have to worry
about the puppy getting out today. She walked down
the path to the front yard and saw the moving truck
that had just backed into the driveway. That must have
been the beeping noise she heard as it backed up. A
Mercedes had pulled to the curb and a small, petite

blonde woman who looked to be somewhere in her fifties stood on the grass, looking at the inn with a mixture of awe and excitement.

She smiled when she saw Nina and crossed the yard. "Hello, I'm Alice McIntyre. I'll be your new neighbor."

Nina smiled. "I'm Nina Hanson. It's nice to meet you. Welcome to the neighborhood. I've been expecting you. And excited to meet you."

"Likewise. Jackson, my son, told me he had met you the other day. He was slightly relieved that I wasn't moving in next door to an ax murderer or serial killer. I'm in your debt for instantly proving him wrong to worry about me like he does. Thank you for reassuring him." Alice's smile was genuine and warm.

Nina could tell Alice adored her son, though there was a definite hint of a strain on the worrying he did. Nina had an instant flashback of a hard body and deep brown eyes and had a feeling Jackson, as Alice had called him, could be intense. Jackson—the name suited him.

"I'm glad he didn't think I'm an ax murderer. Although he didn't ask me any personal questions, so he really doesn't know for certain, and I have a feeling he'll realize this soon and come to give me a thorough interrogation."

Alice smiled, and her blue eyes twinkled. "You've

only just met him briefly and already you've got him figured out. My oldest son can be overprotective. And to say that he's not being overly protective right now would be an understatement. I didn't even tell him I was buying this property until I had the deed in my name. As you've determined from your first encounter, he's a little nervous."

"I did get that idea. Kept talking about security and traffic. It's a quiet area, for the most part. The island police are a solid presence, though it's a very laid-back small town. As safe as you'll find. I walk almost everywhere when I'm in town."

"I came by yesterday and walked to town. It's one of the things I enjoy. Jackson said you'd been here about three years, so you should know. I'm so looking forward to that. My lawyer did a background check on it before the purchase and it's just like I remembered it from when I worked here many years ago in the summer. I'm excited to be here, to enjoy the atmosphere again and to throw myself into this renovation."

The fact that Jackson had remembered all the details of their brief conversation pleased her. She wasn't sure exactly why, but it did. The wistfulness was clear in Alice's words and the way she looked at the inn. "I think you opening the inn is a great idea. There are several bed-and-breakfasts in town and the hotels, though not that many because there just isn't the land for it. It's what helps keep the charm, you know?"

"And that is another reason I'm so glad to be here. The beach here is wonderful, and I love the access. And the back veranda is amazing, overlooking the beach. Once upon a time, this inn was a glorious place, full of hospitality and charm. I want to bring that back. And it will be so good for me. I lost my husband last year and I've felt so lost. Like a sailboat without a sail, I'm a bit stuck." She waved toward the inn. "Star Gazer Inn is a new beginning for me."

Nina's heart ached for Alice, and she suddenly understood some of Jackson's overprotective instincts now. His mother was grieving and searching to find her footing again. He, too, was probably doing the same thing, especially as the oldest son. Her heart went out to him and the responsibility he must feel.

"It is still beautiful. I'm going to be quite happy here. I've been living on our ranch since I was nineteen and my William, the love of my life, married me and carried me over the threshold. It was a wonderful life out there, raising my boys, but it was time for a change and the boys don't need me at the ranch. Sometimes a girl just needs the beach."

Nina felt a deep pang of regret for her neighbor at being a widow. She hated to think of anyone losing the love of their life and being in the situation of having to restart life without them. It wasn't a pleasant thought at all. And Alice was right; Nina understood all too well that the beach was just something a girl needed at certain times in her life.

It seemed that for Alice, this was that time.

Just as it was for her, also.

"Did you find anything interesting when you were shopping?" Nina asked, being conversational and truly interested in what Alice was going to do to the inn.

"I found a few decoration items. I'm going to hire a contractor to start painting and updating the bathrooms. I'll do some painting in a few rooms and decorate. What are your favorite shops in town for some inspiration pieces?"

Nina didn't hesitate. "Mary Lou's is fantastic. Anything specific you're looking for?"

"You know, traditional B&B type items to spread around. But I'd love to find some local artwork for the rooms. I saw several galleries. I checked out a few but so far haven't seen anything that's reached out and spoke to me, you know? I'll keep checking back. I'll find what I'm looking for in a new piece."

Nina bit her lip.

Alice caught her hesitation. "You look like you've thought of something."

"If you don't find anything, let me know. I have a

few paintings I could show you."

Alice's eyes widened at the offer. "You're an artist? How wonderful. I'd love to see your work. I'm looking for just the right thing, so it might not fit what I'm hoping to find but I'd love to look."

She was going to have a problem if Alice liked the paintings. *Why had she offered, anyway? Too late now.* "I'll bring some things over for you to look at. Or, I can pull some things out for you to see or you can come over to my cottage later and take a look."

"Perfect. You just tell me what time and I'll be there."

"Perfect." She shouldn't be showing anyone her paintings. Hadn't shown her work in over three years. So why had she spoken up when the possibility loomed that it was a mistake?

* * *

Jackson was running late as he pulled up to the curb and parked behind his mother's Mercedes. The moving truck was still there, which he was glad for. He'd had a sleepless night. The recurring nightmares that had plagued him since his dad drowned in the Frio River while they were moving cattle on their ranchland near Bandera had hit relentlessly last night. He'd been moving slow, and it had taken a pot of coffee to get his sluggish brain working this morning. Then he'd had a call about their upcoming cattle sale and charity event at the end of next month and it had taken up more time than he'd allotted.

Now, he hopped from his truck and he hurried toward the back of the inn, glancing toward the house next door as he went. And wondered if his mother had met her new neighbor yet. Thoughts of her had crossed his mind several times over the last couple of days, remembering those moments they'd talked. He wondered whether he had appeared brusque with her, too harsh. The possibility bothered him. He'd had a lot on his mind but that didn't excuse any sharpness he might have had in his tone.

He'd just been uptight about what his mother had done, but that was no excuse either. Walking up the driveway past the moving van, he saw two guys moving a couch in through the back way. He had seen on his visit the day before that the back porch had several doorways; as a matter of fact, a set of French doors opened up into a large, bright and cheerful living space that was in full view of the beach and the bay. He walked in that direction, the blue of the water glistening as he rounded the edge and stepped up onto the deck.

The colorful Adirondack chairs, faded but welcoming, sat on the wide veranda. He walked through the enormous glass French doors that were open wide to the living space where the moving men were setting the couch.

He was startled to see the pretty neighbor talking with his mother. They were concentrating on where to position the couch and didn't see him at first so he waited by the door.

His mom brightened when she caught sight of him, then looked back at the couch that the men had repositioned to her specifications. "That's perfect, guys. Now for the two chairs." The men left to get the chairs from the van, and she turned to him. "Jackson, I'm so glad you're here. This is so exciting! Nina, this is Jackson, my oldest son. I know that you two met already but haven't been officially introduced, I don't believe. She's an artist and does gorgeous work."

An artist. "Hi, it's nice to see you again." He removed his hat, something he had not done two days ago. But then again, he had his arms full of a puppy. He held his hand out and Nina placed her hand in his, and suddenly he was very interested in his mother's move much more than he had been. His interest sparked higher as Nina's soft hazel eyes met his. She was even prettier today than he remembered her from two days ago.

"Likewise. It's nice to meet you, officially." She smiled.

There was a smudge of white paint visible on her left cheek, which made sense if she was an artist. His finger suddenly itched to wipe that paint off her cheek and feel her soft skin beneath the rough pad of his thumb. He returned her smile and reluctantly released her hand. "I'm at a loss to figure out how someone can take a paintbrush and create something of beauty on a canvas. It isn't in my wheelhouse, but I'm amazed by the talent of others."

"Your mother will make this into a beautiful place."

"I've already started with your gorgeous beachscape. Look at the painting." His mother moved to stand beside a large covered painting leaning against the wall. "Isn't this gorgeous?" She looked at Jackson as she lifted the sheet from the painting.

Jackson stared at the painting of a brilliant sunset, the view from a porch with a rose-pink bougainvillea trailing from a trellis. The colors were amazing. "Wow. You painted this?"

"I did."

He slid his gaze from the painting to Nina and found her studying him. "Like I said, I'm amazed by talented people. I love the colors. Though I tend to go to the muted side of things."

"I love color. My home is decorated vibrantly. Color lights up the world. So is brown your favorite color?" There was humor in her eyes and her lips twitched.

She read him like an open book. "Yup. But I like the color of green grass and I like blue oceans and I like the color of hay and good brown earth. Dark wood and tans—that's me. But I think I can get used to a little color."

His mother chuckled. "When you come here, you'll have to, Jackson. I'm letting my bright side out here at the inn."

She looked happily at him, and his heart twisted with love for this woman he held high above all others. "This is good for you, Mom. You look happy."

"I am." She looked at Nina. "Jackson holds our family together. He's adaptable, and I think maybe he's going to enjoy coming here and watching me adapt. You'll have to come over often, Nina. And bring that cute puppy."

"I'll do that. And speaking of Buttercup, I better go check on her. She was sleeping in her pen but it's time for her to get outside and play. You two have a great day. And, honestly, Alice, if you need anything, just ask."

And with that, she walked out the door, passing the moving men on their way back inside, each carrying a blue chair. He watched her until she was out of sight and then found his mother watching him with keen interest.

"Just put those there at the end of the couch. Thank you." She directed the men then turned her curious gaze to him again. "She's a great gal. Might be someone you want to spend some time with."

"Mother, don't start trying to fix me up with your neighbor."

She laughed and stuck her arm through his, interlacing them as she laid her head on his shoulder and squeezed hard. His heart squeezed just as hard.

"I love you, Jackson. But, son, it's time for you to lighten up. And, honestly, you need some color in your life, just as much as I do. And for you, I'm not talking about a painting."

CHAPTER FIVE

Nina hurried from the Star Gazer Inn, her heart pounding. It was still beating a rapid drum roll as she entered her house and closed the door firmly behind her. She could still feel the roughness of Jackson's hand clasping hers. His hand had enclosed hers and she hadn't pulled away, hadn't flinched. Hadn't recoiled.

Instead, she had been lost in the pull of his mesmerizing eyes as he'd studied her with an interest that intrigued her.

And she could have none of that.

Breathing deeply, set on getting control of her runaway pulse, she counted to ten then pushed away from the wall and headed toward the laundry room.

Jackson was wealthy beyond anything she could imagine. Could that be the reason she hadn't reacted negatively? He had enough money that she didn't have to worry whether he was a two-timing swindler out to make a fool out of her.

Would she ever be able to get over her past and not be wary of all men?

She opened the door of the laundry where Buttercup slept. She would take the puppy on a walk down the beach. But her thoughts were still locked on Jackson. He was easy to think about, especially because she could see the affection between him and his mother. That, too, was reassuring. Surely a guy that concerned about his mother was a good guy.

She liked his mother. When Alice had come over and looked at her artwork, they'd sat on her porch and had a cup of coffee. They had talked about Alice's plans for the inn, and she was so excited about what she was planning that it was contagious. Then she'd learned she was the late wife of the well-known, wealthy rancher William McIntyre. In these parts, the name was very familiar. Even to a newcomer of three years like herself, it was common knowledge that the McIntyres were generous with their wealth and every charity, fundraiser, and high school benefited from donations or scholarships from the family.

And now Alice was becoming an innkeeper. It

was mind-boggling. Wasn't every day that the heiress of billions and one of the largest ranches in the state of Texas, and probably one of the most oil-wealthy, was now her next-door neighbor. And now the owner of the quaint inn that probably didn't even hold a candle to the home that she knew existed on the McIntyre Ranch. A massive home that had been featured in many magazines over the years and even once used as the backdrop for a movie. Though she didn't pay attention to all of that, everyone around this area knew of the McIntyre family. Just like they knew of the King Ranch and several others in this area between Corpus Christi and San Antonio, each huge and owned by men like Jackson McIntyre.

Buttercup jumped up and wiggled from top to bottom of her curly caramel-colored body.

"Hey, girl, let's go for a walk." She walked into the kitchen as the puppy clamored at her feet. She opened the refrigerator and pulled out the glass pitcher of homemade lemonade. Pulling a red insulated mug from the upper cabinet, she poured lemonade into it, snapped the lid into place and walked toward the glass doors leading out onto the patio. Reaching up, she plucked the leash from the hook and then bent down and snapped it to Buttercup's collar. She opened the door, and they headed outside into the sunlight. She loved walking on the beach and Buttercup strained at the end of the leash as they crossed the sand to the water. A seagull chased another seagull overhead and Buttercup jumped into the air, barking at them. She laughed and was so glad she had Buttercup.

She'd lived a solitary life for the last three years and a lonely life here on the island. The feel of Jackson's hand on hers caused a longing she hadn't expected. And as she walked along the breezy, beautiful blue coast, she wondered what might happen with future meetings. She didn't have to wait long. When she was walking back to her house, she saw a tall, lean figure standing beside the water. He was holding his cowboy hat in his hand and it rested against his thigh. Butterflies fluttered in her chest— and she fought them off like they were life-sucking mosquitoes. This would not do. She thought about angling up the beach toward her house and not continuing along the water's edge that would take her straight to him. But then he turned and looked straight at her. And Buttercup raced toward him startling her so much that she let go of the leash.

"Buttercup," she called and hurried after the golden, growing ball of fur. The pup danced with delight, jumping up and greeting Jackson. He bent and picked up the leash while petting her dog.

"Thank you," she said when she reached him. "It seems like you're always catching my dog."

"I'm honored to help to keep the little gal out of trouble." He handed her the leash and continued to pet Buttercup's head as she had her paws on his thigh.

"I just haven't gotten comfortable trusting her not to run off and getting lost. She's very curious."

"Totally a good idea."

They stared at each other then and neither one of them said anything. She was trying to figure out what to say and he just seemed comfortable staring at her. It was disconcerting.

"Look, I was leaving Mom's and I got to thinking that maybe we should exchange phone numbers." Her expression must have relayed how startling his suggestion was because he quickly added, "In case something happened, and Mom needed me. You could contact me. Or if I needed to contact you in case I might need you to check on her. If you didn't mind doing that."

She relaxed, though she felt a pang of regret that he wasn't asking for her number because he wanted it for more personal reasons. Again, she buried this thought with a thousand reasons why she shouldn't want him wanting to get to know her on a personal level.

"Sure, that's a good idea. Although I'm not sure if you know this, but your mother is not that old and she seems extremely capable of taking care of herself." He was really protective of Alice and while she thought that was sweet for a son to worry about his mother it was also, in his case, maybe a bit over the top. Then again it wasn't really her business.

"I know you're right. But I'd rather be safe than sorry. And I'd do it because I love my mom but also because my dad would want me too."

She understood. She held her hand out. "Let me have your phone."

He placed his phone in her hand and she pulled up his phone app and tapped the new contact screen and filled in her name and number. "This is not to be shared with anyone else," she said as she handed it back to him. "Now, call me and I'll have your info.

"I wouldn't ever share this with anyone." He tapped the new number and her phone rang.

She took the call then immediately ended it. Then tapped new contact and filled his name in. She stared at the information realizing this was the first new contact she'd placed in her phone in over three years. She looked up and he smiled at her. She didn't smile back. She hadn't given her number to anyone since Joe. And handing it out to a man, especially after Joe, was the last thing she'd ever expected to do.

"I need to go. But I promise if for any reason I need to contact you about your mother, I'll call you."

"Thanks."

"Come on, Buttercup." She started toward her house, pulling the dog gently as she had to encourage her to leave Jackson behind. Nina understood the reluctance to leave him all too well.

"Nina," he called, his deep voice ringing out over the breeze off the ocean.

She turned to find him exactly where she'd left him. "Yes."

"Is everything alright?"

"Yes, why would you ask?"

"I don't know, you seem sometimes afraid of me, or wary. Am I reading that vibe correctly?"

Her heart jumped at how clearly he'd read her reactions to him. Well most of her reactions, thankfully he might not have read her disturbing attraction to him. "No. I'm just not good with new acquaintances. Have a good day." She turned and hurried across the sand hoping he didn't ask more questions.

* * *

A week after his mother had moved off the ranch, Jackson rode on the barge as it ferried the cattle across the intercoastal to the small island named Whisper Cove across from their property on the mainland where they grazed cattle. This was one of the few areas that had no access by vehicles, but the barge worked fine.

Had been used by their family for decades.

He watched the land draw near as his thoughts roamed to Nina as they'd done all week. She intrigued him.

Something hummed in the air between them when they were in a room together, but she was ignoring it. When he'd been there on moving day, he'd gotten the impression that she'd used checking on her dog as an excuse to get away from him. He wasn't exactly used to a woman giving him a semi-cold shoulder. It wasn't blatant, but it was subtle, and it bugged him. Was she attracted to him, like he suspected, and not wanting to be?

Maybe she just didn't want to be attracted to anyone. He told himself not to take it personally, but he was and there was no denying that it bothered him. He wasn't particularly happy to be interested in the woman who would be his mother's neighbor. It complicated things, and right now everything was complicated enough. Already his mother had hinted at him and Nina getting together. He didn't need his mother matchmaking. She wanted grandchildren, and he felt the pressure. He didn't need her pushing her poor neighbor to go out with him. Maybe that was the issue. It was a lightbulb moment. Maybe his mother had already started pushing him on Nina, and that was why she'd practically run from the house after he'd shown up.

And why the next two days that he'd gone over to make sure the security system was being taken care of, she had been nowhere in sight. He had hired the best security company in Corpus Christi. He'd used them before and knew there was no need to oversee what they were doing. He'd used them as an excuse to go to the inn, in hopes of seeing Nina. But her car hadn't been in sight either day, and he didn't feel like asking his mother whether she had seen her. That would really have had Alice's ears perking up. But, then again, his mother had been preoccupied with lists and paint colors, and there were pieces of different colored material strewn all over the kitchen island. Said she was getting her color palette ready and would need a contractor soon.

Instead of talking about Nina, he'd made calls about a contractor.

She was meeting them today, he thought, and was going to pick one. He'd only chosen the best, so hopefully she would like one of them.

Tucker came to the front of the barge to stand beside him. Cattle shifted and mooed as his brother placed his hands on the railing and then his gaze landed on Jackson.

"What are you thinking about? You were a thousand miles away." Tucker leaned against the rail.

"Why do you say that?"

"Because I called your name twice, and you didn't hear me."

"We're on a barge full of bawling cattle."

"Never stopped you from hearing me before. What's up?"

It was true; he had spectacular hearing. They always teased him that his kids weren't going to be able to ever say anything they didn't want him to hear. He gave his brother a squint-eyed appraisal. "I guess you were right. I was deep in thought."

"Well? About what? You've been doing that a lot the last couple days. Is this thing with Mom moving out really got you tied up in knots?"

"Yeah, it does, but I'm adjusting. But I'm worried about her. When are you going to go over there and see the place? It's going to be nice when she's finished with it. I talked to her this morning and she said she was up to her armpits in color swatches and paint chips right now. Jewel tones, she calls them—oranges, pinks, purples, blues of every shade imaginable. Brilliant colors, no brown or tan in sight."

Tuck looked at him as if he were talking an unfamiliar language. "You mean like bright colors?"

Jackson laughed, feeling his brother's pain. "Yeah, real bright. It's a new day dawning over there. That inn is not going to look anything like the ranch with all its Texas cattle country shades of brown."

"No leather and that black granite in the kitchen that Dad always loved—said it looked great with the walnut wood?"

"The kitchen is white and it's going to stay that color. It's nice and bright, and with those big windows overlooking the ocean, that beautiful blue of the Corpus Christi Bay just hits you in the face. She seems happier just being there."

They were both silent as they watched the land drawing closer as the barge made its way toward the dock.

Jackson finally spoke again. "This is what she needs. Her eyes are alive for the first time since before…" He didn't need to finish the sentence. Their lives were defined now and forever by *before* their dad's death and *after* his death.

"That's a good thing," Tucker said quietly as their gazes met. "As long as she's happy, I'm okay with anything she wants to do. It's just different."

"Yes." Jackson knew exactly what Tucker was thinking. They were just going to have to adjust to their mom spreading her wings some and trying new things. "You know, I've been thinking about it. She married Dad when she was barely twenty. He was, what, six years older than her, and they moved out here to the ranch and that's where her life has been all these years. She has to be a little scared, I think, but she's not showing it. I could be wrong, but a new beginning takes courage and I think that's where she's at right now."

Tucker's face was all hard lines as he stared straight ahead. Finally, his shoulders relaxed. "Yeah, so I guess I'm going to go over there and see this new adventure for myself. Show Mom my support. Not that I didn't offer her my help with the remodeling in the beginning, but she told me she was hiring a contractor for the renovation needs and she was going shopping for furniture and could do that on her own. I got the feeling she didn't want me over there."

Jackson got that same feeling. "She knows how busy we are with the ranch, and she's spreading her wings and although she wants us to visit, I think starting this new chapter in her life is something she doesn't need us looking over her shoulder while she's doing it. Still, I'm going over there tomorrow. Whether she wants me to or not, I'll be checking on her at least once a week. If you fellas go around some too, then we can make sure everything is going along smoothly for her."

"She may tell us to get lost if we start smothering her." Tucker looked skeptical.

"She'll have to get used to us checking on her, because that's just the way it's going to be."

CHAPTER SIX

Riley stood on the coast, the section of the ranch that had a long-deserted expanse of beautiful beach access that he had had on his mind for weeks now. It had happened because of the chance encounter at a gas station. He had been traveling, hauling cattle down to central Texas, and stopped to fill his hauler up with gas. The gas tank was spending his money with the speed of light when a cherry-red Jeep Cherokee pulled up at the pump across from him. It was pulling the cutest little camper trailer he had ever seen. It was one of those vintage jobs that looked like an off-centered teardrop. It was painted a soft pink, with turquoise lettering on the side that spelled "Live, Laugh, Love and Enjoy Life… It's just too dang short."

But that wasn't what caught his attention. It was the vibrant redhead who sprang from the Jeep with endless legs that were stuffed into cowboy boots and cut-off shorts. She smiled at him, then strode around to the other side of the Jeep and fed the machine her credit card. Her thick red hair had bounced with every purposeful step she'd taken.

And he'd stood there, stunned silent. But not for long. "Nice ride."

She looked at him as she put the gas nozzle into the gas tank. "Thank you. Me and my little Tootsie-Roller are travelin' partners. We love road trippin' adventures."

He laughed and walked around to lean against the fender of his truck so he could be closer to her. "I bet you two have some stories to tell." He crossed his arms and enjoyed the view of that beautiful smile and eyes as green as an emerald in sunlight.

She watched him across the top of her vehicle, then she grabbed the windshield wand and started cleaning bugs from her windshield. "Yes, we do. Most definitely."

He pushed away from his truck and strode to stand across the hood of the Jeep from her. He held out his hand. "I'll grab this side if you want me to."

She eyed him suspiciously with very intelligent

eyes.

He held up his hands. "I promise I'm no stalker, no serial killer, just a cowboy gettin' some gas and trying to help a pretty lady clean buggy windows so she and her 'Tootsie-Roller' can get on down the road for another adventure."

She laughed with delight and handed him the cleaning wand. "Thank you. Knock yourself out."

"I thought you'd never ask." He scrubbed the windshield on his side. "So what do you do with this cute road trippin' buddy of yours?"

"Glamping. It was a great weekend with a bunch of my girlfriends."

He stopped scrubbing. "Did you say 'glamping,' with a G?"

"Yes, you heard correctly. We pick a place on the map every month or quarter. We don't always get to make it to every adventure, but there are a lot of us so we have a planned trip and everyone who can shows up."

"So what is the difference in 'glamping' versus 'camping'?"

"Oh, that G is very important." Her eyes twinkled, and when she laughed, it was as if the clouds parted and a sunbeam shined down on them.

He was completely smitten. He had never been instantaneously drawn to someone like that, but this woman was amazing.

"Glamping with a G stands for glamour and camping combined. You know, men like to go camping and get all hunting and shooting and getting sweaty then sleeping on the ground. We women have our own way of doing things. We do it glamorously. Our campers have beds in them and even a little kitchen, though we don't cook while glamping. The glamping venues are very nice facilities. They provide gourmet meals, spa treatments so we can have massages, our nails and toes done and facials. There's champagne, wine and tea and coffee—you know, all the essentials. We get to sit around and be treated like queens all weekend. It's an amazing, fun-filled, delightful time. Men don't understand it at all."

He wanted to understand it. It sounded like something he could see women enjoying. "I think it sounds cool. Not that I want to do it, but I can see women doing that. My mom would probably love that. Not that she's gone camping in a very long time, but you know, she is a mother of four men and I'm sure there's been a time or two that she would have wanted a weekend away like that."

"Your mother raised four sons like you?"

"Yeah, she's a saint." He handed her back the handle of the windshield cleaner and their fingertips brushed and there was a spark. Of course, he already knew there would be a spark; he felt a spark from the moment he saw her. "You say that like it's a terrible thing."

She laughed again. "Not at all. It's just that I was raised an only child. I can't imagine having brothers or sisters, although I have to say I think it would have been nice to have siblings. But four, probably very mischievous, boys? She's more than likely a very strong woman."

He thought about his mom. "Pretty much. She's wonderful. My dad died about a year and a half ago and really, she's been a rock, but we've all worried about her. She just doesn't seem like herself. But she's going to make it. This glamping thing, I might have to check into that for her. Tell me about these places y'all go."

"We try to stick to Texas. You know, Texas is a big state and there's a lot of us. Some of us are younger and some of us are older, there are a lot of widows too. We try to stick to where everybody can meet. It's easy to look—you can Google it and you'll pull it up. Our group is called 'Glamping We Shall Do.' Just type that in and you'll see what's on our agenda—not that I'm asking you to be a stalker or anything. If you wanted to get your mom a little camper and she was interested in joining, she could do that—just sign on through the website. The lady who runs it would be glad to help."

She pulled the nozzle out of the gas tank and replaced the lid, then placed the nozzle back in the gas pump. She smiled at him. "Anyway, I've got to go got—a lot of traveling to do before I reach home. Good luck. It's nice talking to you." And she got in her vehicle.

He stepped back, waved, and watched her slowly pull out of the station and disappear.

And he had not been able to get her off his mind in the month since that encounter. He had looked up Glamping We Shall Do, and it had been impressive. He had checked out the places that they glamped and the idea had sparked that they had the perfect place for a venue. He had done a lot of things in his lifetime to impress a woman, but this particular woman—he had not gotten her name; she had not offered it—she was a safety conscious woman. She had not given him her name even though he had helped her. He admired her for that. He had a feeling she probably had a gun inside that vehicle with her, too. Women who traveled alone? Yup. Texas woman? Oh yeah, he had a feeling this little gal could take care of herself. And though she had been pleasant, and they had had that little connection, she still had not let her guard down and had not given her name. Of course, he could have taken her license plate number, but he hadn't. He wasn't into tracking people down through information he didn't have any business using, even though he had a friend in the police department.

But he looked around the sandy shores of the McIntyre Ranch and he saw it just as clear as the day he had gotten the idea. He was going to do this.

* * *

At the end of her first week, Alice was settling into the inn. Her spirits were up as she picked up her mug of morning coffee and walked out onto the back porch. She had a sense of purpose with all the plans that filled her mind for the inn. It felt good. She'd even been sleeping better since moving here. Oh, she wasn't sleeping great yet, just better. She'd begun having insomnia right after William died. It was to be expected, because she longed to have him beside her again and she missed him so very much. Still did. That would never change. But with time, one would think sleeping would get easier. And for some widows and widowers it might, but it hadn't gotten better for her. She paced the ranch house at night, or sat and read, or stared out at the moon. She did a lot of things at night, but sleeping just wasn't one of them.

But the last few nights, she'd gone to bed with her thoughts full of plans and with a sense of wellbeing that she hadn't felt before. The first night, despite being thrilled with her choice to open the inn, she had cried herself to sleep. Moving on into a future without the love of her life beside her was so very difficult. But amid her tears, she could hear William telling her to get on with it. "Darlin', I'm long gone and I'm not coming back. It's time for you to get on with it and begin a new life for yourself. Go for it. Dream big and be happy."

Be happy. She'd lain there, staring up at the white ceiling, her heart squeezed so tight she could barely breathe as she saw his handsome face looking down at her. He had been such a handsome cowboy. They'd stared at each other for the longest moment and then his face had disappeared, but his smile had lingered on in her heart.

Blinking back tears, she breathed deeply of the ocean air, let the heat of the morning sun warm the chill from her as she walked around the house, studying the flower beds. She loved flowers and watching them grow and flourish. As she walked to the front of the inn and the large, very much in need of some love flower bed, she knew this was the one would tackle first. And tomorrow was the day she planned to start. She knew exactly what she would plant. Knew exactly the appearance of the inn she wanted as her guests drove up. She had met with two different contractors the day before and both had perfect references, but she hadn't hired either of them. She hoped she found her contractor soon so things would start moving along.

A sound from next door drew her attention. She turned to see Nina and Buttercup coming her way. Buttercup was straining at her leash to get to her.

Alice knelt and set her coffee cup on the grass, then caught Buttercup in her arms. The puppy was growing and adorable. She had been thinking all week she might want a dog but with the inn, she wasn't sure whether she should have a dog in her quarters in case it would bother her guests—maybe barking or whether a guest had allergies.

"She is so cute." She smiled up at Nina.

"She loves you but please don't let her get you dirty."

"She's not. Are you going somewhere?" She saw Nina's small purse strapped across her body.

"Yes, we were on our way to the car and then heading to a flea market they're having downtown this morning."

"Oh really, a flea market? Are you looking for company?"

Nina's expression was jubilant. "Sure. I came to ask if you might want to go. It should be fun and worth the drive. You never know what treasures await you."

"So true. This is exciting. Let me put my coffee mug in the house and grab my purse and sunshades, and I'm ready to roll."

* * *

Nina chuckled as she watched Alice hurry away, seeming so thrilled about the flea market. It was going to be fun. She hadn't spent time with anyone like this in so very long and it was a stark reminder of how isolated she'd kept herself these three years. Not today, she was thrilled Alice had agreed to come with her. She needed girl time. Even more than she'd realized.

Moments later, they piled into her Mini Cooper and she put the top down. It was a gorgeous day. Buttercup sat in her seat with her harness on, fastened in, and had her tongue hanging out, happily lapping at the wind as they headed over the bridge to the downtown.

"I'm so glad you came along," she said over the wind. "I haven't really made a lot of friends since I moved here. My fault, I've just kept to myself these past few years."

"You should have been getting involved in things in town and making friends."

"True, but I've been a hermit instead."

"That makes me extra glad you asked me to come

along. Anything in particular you're looking for?"

"No, I don't always buy stuff. I just enjoy looking, and when I see a piece that speaks to me, I grab it. It's just a hobby I have. How about you?"

Alice smiled and looked thoughtful. "When I was a girl, my mother was a single parent, and we didn't have a lot of money and so we did a lot of flea marketing. We would go every Friday to garage sales and Saturdays to flea markets. And she loved finding 'treasures,' as she called them. It was just fun and a great time to bond with my mother. You know, looking back on it, my mom probably never paid much for anything we ever bought. But it was just a fun experience, and I love that memory. Every time I think about a flea market, I think about my mom."

"I like that. So you've gone to flea markets a lot?"

"Not since I was a girl."

"Oh, why not?"

"The ranch house wasn't really the flea market kind of place. We had a distinct decorating style. A lot of leather and beautiful polished wood."

"I saw your home in a magazine once. It was gorgeous."

"Thank you. I loved it, but that isn't the style I have in mind for the inn. I need something lighter. Something that's bright and beachy."

"I get it. You're going back to your roots." She

glanced at Alice as she pulled into the parking lot. Her new friend looked suddenly sad. "Is something wrong?" She pulled into a parking space and turned off the engine, then gave Alice her full attention. She looked a little pale.

"You are exactly right. I love my home at the ranch. Loved every moment I was there with William and my boys. But since I lost William, my heart has been so broken that being there without him has been hard. This inn is me running away, putting some distance between me and my memories I wanted to hold on to so very, very much." She sighed. "But I couldn't do it." Alice's lip trembled. "But I feel guilty for taking this step, even knowing William would approve."

Tears welled in Nina's eyes for the pain Alice was feeling and because she understood it all too well. "I'm so very sorry for your loss."

Alice sniffed and bit her lip as she bravely gave a trembling smile. "Thank you. And like I said, this is what William would want. This is me not trying to get away but spreading my wings."

"Which is a good thing to do and much needed. Don't feel bad. You have to do what you have to do to make that heart smile again."

Alice stared at her. "Why do I feel that you're saying that as someone who knows?"

She knew she had said too much, but she couldn't help it. "Because I'm also a widow. A little different circumstance, I think. I wasn't married as long as you were, but I was still a little bit lost, so I understand, you know. Not everybody gets that."

Alice squeezed Nina's hand. "I'm so sorry. You're far too young to have gone through the loss of your husband. My condolences. You're going to have to tell me about him."

"I will but right now I didn't mean to bring our conversation down. Let's go check out this flea market. It's going to be fun. And I have a feeling that we're both going to find something spectacular today."

Alice smiled. "I think you're absolutely correct. Let's do this."

Nina laughed, let Buttercup out of the car and followed Alice into the crowd.

CHAPTER SEVEN

Jackson pulled into the driveway of the inn around five and was surprised when Nina pulled into her driveway with his mom in the passenger seat. She waved at him and motioned for him to come over. He climbed out of his truck and strode across the yard to see where they had been. He had hoped he would see Nina today, so this was a welcomed surprise.

"Hey ladies, looks like you've been off somewhere fun."

Nina smiled at him as she got out of the car. "We had such a wonderful time, and you are just the person we need."

"Jackson, it was so fun." His mom's expression was jubilant as he opened her door for her. She hugged him as soon as she was on her feet. "I'm so glad you're here. We need you. Come back here to the back. We've had the most wonderful afternoon at the local flea market. I found some great buys but I've realized that not being at the ranch that I need to get a bigger car or a truck because I have to go back and pick up all the things I couldn't carry. But we have several boxes you can help us carry inside."

"Here I was hoping you'd be happy to see me because I'm your favorite son."

His mom laughed. "That too. There's always that. You know you're my favorite son."

"You tell us all that."

"Yes, but y'all aren't supposed to know that."

"We compare notes, Mom."

Nina chuckled. "Sounds like an age-old debate."

He squinted at her in the sun. "Yes, it is. My three brothers believe her. I try to tell them she says that to everybody. But they each believe that she means it for only them."

His mother laughed. "I do mean it. Y'all are all my favorite sons. Anyway, grab that box."

There were two mid-sized boxes stuffed side by side in the back of the very tiny vehicle. Nina had let her dog climb out of the backseat and it was wiggling at his feet now, with its leash fastened securely to its collar. He reached down and scratched the puppy behind its ear. "Hello to you too. Have they asked you to carry anything yet?" The dog barked and wagged its fuzzy tail. "Aha. I take that as a no. So doggy labor isn't allowed?" he asked Nina.

She was watching him with eyes lit with humor. "Nope. You're it, if you don't mind."

"I don't mind a bit. Where do you want these?" He looked from Nina to his mother.

"You help Nina. I'm going to go over to the house and put some coffee on. Bring my box over after you're done. No hurry at all." She started across the yard and looked over her shoulder. "Nina, I had a fantastic time and we're going to do this again soon. Come over when Jackson comes over. I'm popping a fresh cinnamon coffee cake into the oven to warm. You'll want some."

Jackson looked at Nina. "You will want some—take my word for it."

She looked hesitantly from him to his mother. "It sounds delicious. I'll be over when Jackson brings the boxes."

After his mother was gone, awkwardness filled the space between them. "Thanks for spending time with my mother. She looked really happy."

He lifted the box into his arms. It was fairly heavy despite not being large.

"No need to thank me for that. I've enjoyed

getting to know your mom, she's awesome and we had a great time. She really had fun at the flea market."

He followed her toward her back door. "I'm glad she did. You've probably already figured out that we're worried about her adjusting to life without my dad and we just expected that she would stay at the ranch. This came out of nowhere, but I have to admit she hasn't looked this happy in a long time."

They reached the side entrance to the house. It had three steps up to a side door; she punched in a code and the lock released. She pushed the door open. "After you."

"I'll wait. You go first." She passed by him and her sweet scent drifted to him as he followed her.

The puppy trotted ahead of Nina but halted suddenly, then spun and raced back to the door and behind Jackson. He halted as Nina spun around to face him, yanked closer as Buttercup proceeded to race past her, causing the leash to wrap behind Jackson's knees. He immediately set the box on the top of the washing machine and grabbed Nina as the dog barked and, with her continuing to hold onto the leash, tugged her against him.

She looked up at him, blushing profusely. "I am so sorry. Buttercup, stop."

He grinned down at her, unable to lie. "I don't mind at all. As a matter of fact, I might need to give

Buttercup a treat after this." His hands grasped her arms gently above the elbows and he flexed his fingers, itching to slide his arms around her. He could feel her heart beating between them and was certain she could feel his doing the same.

As if in answer to believing she deserved a treat, Buttercup barked, sat on her haunches, and looked up at him with a grin.

He really liked this little golden pup. "I might have jumped to conclusions the other day, seeing as how your dog is earning its keep after all." He couldn't help teasing her as he continued to enjoy the feel of her in his arms and the pretty blush of her skin as her gaze drew him to wanting more than he should at that moment.

The hallway was a narrow utility room with a washer and dryer on one side and a dog crate on the other. And the perfect spot for an impromptu ambush by Buttercup.

Still not having said a word, Nina wrapped the arm clutching the leash behind his back and for a moment, he thought she was hugging him as she wrapped the other arm around him.

She made the transfer of the leash handle to her empty hand with the deftness of an Olympic relay runner exchanging a baton. Then she backed away with the speed of a racer ready to fly, and just like that, they were untangled in the quick exchange.

He let her go, regretfully, but respectfully.

"I, on the other hand, need to have a discussion with her about good manners." She smiled as she turned and led the way into the kitchen.

With a quiet sigh, he picked up the box and followed her. The kitchen wasn't huge but it was open to the dining area and living space. The room was washed in light from the large windows and French doors leading onto the patio. Much like the veranda of the inn, he could see the blue of the ocean and an abundance of flowers in the garden separating the house from the white sand.

He set the box on the counter. "Nice place. Is this where you want it?"

She had walked to the other side of the island, putting it between them. "Yes, thank you." She unhooked Buttercup's leash and hung it on a hook beside the door. Buttercup walked over to a dog pillow by the small fireplace and curled up with her chin on her paws. The pup stared at him a minute, then closed her eyes.

"She's tired. We walked her to death today, shopping. And I found out walking a dog on a leash is hard when the dog is curious about every little thing."

"I bet. I can't imagine trying to manhandle my two on a leash."

"But I need to get her used to it in case she has to travel with me long distance."

"I understand. Like I said, my cattle dogs, they have great manners and respond to my commands. But if I put them on a leash, they'd rebel."

She smiled, and the room tension eased. "I totally get it. So are you ready?"

Curious about her, he scanned the room. The house was a deep red and the interior was a soft lemon tone with white trim. The old wood floors were scarred with age and a very light, almost whitewashed pine look. Her furniture was also wood that looked as if it had been white then scrubbed down to the wood, with bits of paint left over. It gave it a worn but homey feel. There were amazing seascapes on the walls and sunsets. The room, though low-keyed tones, was washed in color from the paintings.

"I like your place. It's nice."

She chuckled. "I bet you thought I was going to have a lot of that robin's-egg blue all over my walls like in your mom's place."

"Well, from the way you were talking the other day, I kind of thought that. Is she really going to leave that room looking like that?"

"I doubt it. She had to have enjoyed teasing you, though. When she gets finished, it's going to be gorgeous."

"I'll take your word for that. I like blue but that blue hurt my eyes."

"I predict you are going to have to make some serious adjustments," she said then laughed.

He liked the sound of her laugh more and more.

* * *

"There you two are." His mother looked happy as her gaze flashed between Jackson and Nina.

Jackson suspected him having been at Nina's was part of his mother's happy, smug expression. He had been set up but he wasn't complaining.

"Coffee cake is coming out of the oven now, and coffee is freshly brewed on the coffee bar there. You two fix your drinks like you like it then sit down at the table and I'll get the cake."

"It smells like heaven," Nina said, bringing a wider smile to his mother's face.

"Doesn't it. I adore this recipe and it's one of Jackson's favorites."

He took two mugs from the cabinet above the coffeemaker. "I cannot lie—I could eat the entire cake myself. But I won't. I'll leave a slice or two for you."

"Thank you so very much for leaving me a piece. And for this." Nina took the mug he handed her.

As they took their coffee to the table, his mother

77

set the delicious sweet cake in the center of the small round breakfast table. He inhaled the scent and anticipated his first bite.

"I was thinking," his mother said as she sat down and started slicing the cake. "Jackson, do you have anything to do this evening? Before you go back to the ranch?"

"No. I came to see you and to help out with anything you needed me to do."

"Perfect. As you can see, I'm still deciding on a contractor and am just going over color choices and materials and the contractor is coming tomorrow so I really need to figure this out and am not going to have time to go back and pick up the furniture for a couple of days. Plus, I'm tired after we walked so much and don't really feel like going back. So I was thinking that while you have the truck here, maybe you could go back to the flea market now, and pick up the furniture pieces I purchased."

"Sure. Whatever you need."

"Nina, maybe you could ride with Jackson to show him where to go pick up my furniture. I would really love to have it here tonight. And they said they would be there until seven. It's only a little after five—you've got plenty of time."

Nina looked at Jackson.

He looked at Nina. He couldn't tell whether she

wanted to say no or yes. This was his mother's little manipulation plan, so he remained silent and let her have her fun.

"That would be great. Buttercup will be sleeping, so I'll leave her home. And like Alice said, it would be nice to have the furniture here, and then you and I can move it in for her."

He liked that idea.

His mother smiled and placed a very large portion of cake on his plate. She smiled at him and he was glad to do his part to see that smile.

"But I get to eat this."

His mother chuckled and sent the plate toward him. "Of course, you do."

"I wouldn't leave here before tasting this." Nina dipped her fork into the piece of coffee cake.

His mother's smile widened. "We'll have to start walking, and on the beach. I need the exercise and it's a good way to meet the neighbors."

"Perfect." Nina didn't waste words as she was too busy eating.

Jackson was busy doing the same thing. It dawned on him that this was what his mom was missing, stuck on that ranch with him and his brothers. She didn't have any interaction with women that much unless she came to town and had lunch with her friends, and maybe she needed more of that now.

CHAPTER EIGHT

Alice was pleased with herself as she watched Jackson and Nina drive out of the driveway together. Today, as she and Nina had spent time together, Alice had felt more and more certain that Jackson needed to spend time with her lovely neighbor. And now he was.

She had walked back to the kitchen and was staring at the color swatches once more, knowing she would have to choose a contractor soon or she would never have an inn to open. She had a meeting with the next contractor tomorrow, and he came highly recommended. Maybe he would be the one who would make her feel comfortable enough to hire him.

The doorbell rang and, wondering whether Nina

and Jackson had come back for something, she hurried to the front door and pulled it open. But it wasn't Jackson or Nina who stood on her front porch; it was a very handsome man with dark hair that was graying at the temples and a rugged, tanned face that looked as if he spent a lot of time outdoors. He had pale-blue eyes that jumped out at a person in contrast to his deep tan. He was stunning.

"Alice McIntyre?"

Alice nodded, then spoke in a delayed response. "Yes, and you are?"

He smiled, and she took in more about him: his strong jawline, his lean build and broad shoulders. And as she took him in, his smile widened, and those azure eyes dazzled her.

"I'm Seth Roark. We have an appointment today. Thank you for allowing it to be this late in the day."

"Oh, my goodness, I absolutely forgot you were coming by today. I was thinking it was tomorrow. I am so glad it was a late appointment, or I might have missed you. Please come in." She backed up and held the door for him.

"Are you sure I'm not imposing? If you need me to come back, I can."

"Not in the least. I'm so happy you are here and that I didn't leave you hanging. As a matter of fact, I have a still-warm coffee cake on the table if you'd like a piece while we discuss my plans for the inn." She was too excited about her plans that she did not want him to leave and was totally willing to use her baking to entice him to stay.

He chuckled, rich and husky. "You do know that no well-intentioned man can resist a warm coffee cake, despite it being very unprofessional to accept such an offer on the first meeting?"

She liked him and smiled warmly. "Maybe this is a test and your next decision determines whether you get the job."

"Now you're messing with my mind, because I'm not sure if the test is to see if I accept the coffee cake or deny it?" He chuckled again and small tremors raced through her stomach.

He was funny. "Mr. Roark, the clock is ticking."

"I sure hope the right decision is accepting your hospitality, because I can smell that coffee cake and it is calling my name."

"Perfect. You have passed the first test." He stepped inside and she closed the door behind him. Smiling, she led the way down the hallway to the kitchen area. "Please have a seat and I'll cut you a piece. Coffee?"

"This is too good to be true. Yes, but I can get it."

"No, it will only take a second." Within seconds, she had his coffee in front of him, along with the silverware and the cake. He looked absolutely happy. She had a sudden memory of William sitting at the table enjoying this very coffee cake.

She refilled her own cup then took the seat she'd been in earlier. She watched his delight as he took his first bite. She took a sip of her coffee and wondered how it was that a simple mixture of flour and butter and water and a few other ingredients could combine to make so many people happy.

"This is as good as my grandmother's. And that is saying something special."

She warmed at the compliment. "And with that, you have made my day."

They stared at each other, and then she sipped her coffee, and he took another bite. He set his fork down and took a drink of his coffee.

"Now, about that renovation. This place is great. I'm interested in what your plans are."

"I have some thoughts. The bathrooms are my main focus. Anyone coming to an inn wants a first-class spa bath experience. And these are a bit antiquated and small. I'll be interested in hearing your thoughts on how to enlarge them."

He looked around the kitchen. "Are you planning on anything in here?"

"I would like to add new countertops and paint, if that could be done fairly quickly. I've got samples there on the counter."

"Do you mind if I take a look?"

"No, please do. When you're ready."

He picked up the plate and stood. "I'll take this with me."

She laughed and, taking her coffee with her, she followed him over to the island, where all of her ideas were spread out. She remained silent as he looked at everything. Beside him, she felt very small, only coming to his shoulder. The very idea of such a thought startled her, and she schooled her thoughts away from how fit and handsome he was. *What was wrong with her?*

"I like the colors. Light and professional." He studied the cabinets again then met her gaze. "This could be done quickly. I could probably have you up and running after three days. The cabinets are well made and stainless is a good professional choice. If the counters come out easily, I can have the new ones in within hours."

"That would be perfect. Once I hire a chef, we'll need time in the kitchen to perfect the dishes, so I'd want it done as soon as possible and then the other rooms would follow."

"I can work with that. However, the bathroom renovations will take longer. Let's go take a look."

"I am hoping that it could be within the next three

months, if possible."

"I don't want to give any unrealistic dates until I see everything. I love this old inn, though. I've liked it ever since I was a kid. I'm glad to see you've bought it and will open it again. You're wise to renovate the bathrooms. If the way to a man's heart is his stomach with good food, then the way to a woman's heart is a spectacular bathroom."

She chuckled. He was absolutely right. "Come this way. I'm now eager to hear your ideas. So far, no one has wowed me and as you can see, I haven't hired anyone. I'm hoping you are the man for the job."

"I plan to do everything in my power to convince you to keep me around."

She paused in the hallway, his words striking her on a personal level. She looked over her shoulder at him and he smiled. She liked his smile. She realized that it had been a long time since she had admired a man's appearance, and she told herself it wasn't anything out of the ordinary because Seth Roark was not your average man. She assumed that every woman had the same reaction she was having to him. Besides, she was in no way thinking of anything about a relationship with a man. She wasn't sure she would ever have the heart to love again.

She stopped at the first-floor bathroom. "There are two bathrooms downstairs. And I need them to be spruced up. I'm thinking that they will need a good bit of work as I'm not happy with their look at all. I really don't think bathrooms on the first floor, other than the one that will be in my private quarters, need to have showers and bathtubs."

"I agree. I'm surprised that these bathrooms are like this here."

"Before the owners turned it into an inn, it was a residence. But, like you, I'd have thought it would have been renovated prior to now."

"Now is the time for your vision. Now for upstairs."

Alice led the way up the stairs, but she already knew that unless his bids were way off the mark, he already had the job.

* * *

Nina sat in the truck as they drove toward the downtown area of Corpus Christi, about a thirty-minute drive from Star Gazer Island. She hadn't expected Alice to send her after the furniture with Jackson. Alice had said she would get one of her sons to pick up the furniture. She had never mentioned Nina going with said son.

Then again, she couldn't really be upset, considering Alice hadn't realized that Jackson was going to show up right when they got home from the flea market. And it was logical for Nina to go along and show Jackson where the furniture was located. The layout of flea markets didn't usually make for easy directions to maneuver through the booths. And if she couldn't help out her new neighbor, what kind of neighbor was she, anyway?

No, the truth was she was just uncomfortable with Jackson McIntyre. Why?

She knew the answer to that question: because she was attracted to the man. It had been over three years since she had felt an attraction to anyone and she was fine with that after what she'd been through. She could be giving him an unfair ranking because she was still not thinking great thoughts about men. But it had been three years, and it was way past time for her to get over it. So with that in mind, she tried to relax. She glanced at him. He was driving, and he hadn't spoken either. Maybe he was just as disgruntled about having to take her along on this trip as she was about having to ride along.

The topaz water sparkled as they went over Harbor Bridge that led into Corpus Christi.

"I used to have a hard time going over tall bridges. This one would have been tough for me."

"It's high. I can understand being wary. You look a little nervous right now." He studied her.

"I still get a little stressed but nothing like it used to be. I've overcome my fear for the most part but still get a little nervous when other people are driving over bridges."

"I understand. But from up here, the harbor looks beautiful. You can see so far."

He was right; they were at the top of the crest, and you could see a very long way. "It's a great view." Needing to change the subject, she focused on him and not the bridge and the water below. Far below. "How are you doing adjusting with your mom's moving to the inn?" She was being nosy, but she couldn't help it.

"I guess it's coming from my dad's death and she's finding her way. I've been reading up on it. I learned that sometimes after losing a spouse, the one left behind will go completely against what they were before their loved one's death. I guess my mom is going back to when she was in high school. My mom met my dad at the inn during her first year of college."

She had told Alice that she was also a widow and now she realized that was something that she couldn't keep from him considering she did have some insight in how a widow behaved from personal experience. "There is some merit to that. It was for me—"

"For you what?" he asked, looking at her as they reached the intersection just as a car pulled out in front of them.

WHAT NEW BEGINNINGS ARE MADE OF

It all happened so fast: Jackson slammed on the brakes while at the same time throwing his arm out to protect her. The reaction from him placing his arm out to protect her was nice. It was obviously an instinct for him. They came to a screeching halt and just barely missed the car that managed to get across the intersection.

"I can't believe that guy ran the red light."

"I can't either. Are you okay?"

Her heart pounded, and she had nearly swallowed her tongue as she had been about to speak. But thank goodness she was fine. And the slamming on the brakes hadn't been hard enough to deploy the airbags, which had been a good thing. Airbags exploding in your face was not all that fun, although it did save most lives. "I'm good. Thank you for paying attention. That could have been bad."

"Yeah, it could have been." He pressed the gas pedal, and they moved forward into a slower lane of traffic. He moved over to the right, put his blinker on, and turned onto the road that would take them to the flea market.

Neither one of them spoke as he drove down the lane and then pulled into the designated parking spot that had a big sign and arrow telling him where to go, which was a good thing considering she didn't offer to tell him. She was still a little more shook up than she wanted to admit. When they parked, she undid her seat belt and tried to breathe easier as she let the panic that had engulfed her for a moment slide away. She was thankful that no flashbacks came. She didn't like thinking of bad experiences. Opening the door, she climbed out and closed the door behind her.

He got out and came around beside her. "You sure you're all right?"

"Yes, I am. So, um, we go that way." She pointed, and they started walking toward the entrance, where flags waved to show the entrance to the flea market behind barriers. They kept cars from moving into the place without permission. "When we get in, we'll get a ticket and then we can drive around to the pickup area to get the two pieces that your mom bought."

"Okay. Sounds good. This looks like it was big."

"It was." The hustle and bustle of the flea market had settled down some but not a great bit. They still had an hour to go and there were people who had just gotten off work who wanted to come and check things out, too. Even though it was a Saturday, some people had had to work.

"I have to say, I've actually never been to a flea market before. It looks like people enjoy them."

She gaped at him. "You've never been to a flea market?"

"No. I tend to spend my time at cattle auctions."

She laughed. "Okay, yes, I guess so. Actually, a flea market and a cattle auction are kind of similar, I think. Except you're checking out all the cattle and when we come to a flea market, we're checking out all the good buys. But hopefully we each come out with what we went for in the first place, plus a lot of good stuff we didn't know we needed."

He stopped and looked at her with a curious expression. "I get it. Mom seemed to enjoy it."

"She loved it. Said she and her mother used to spend a lot of time at weekend sales and flea markets growing up. She was like a kid in the candy store. Before we almost had the accident back there, I was about to tell you that I know it might be hard on you and your brothers but if she's had a hard time moving forward after your dad died, this is her way of trying to make the move. Doesn't mean it's easy, though. It might just mean she needed to do it."

He studied her. "How do you know that? Did you go through something similar with your parents?"

She hesitated, not having been this upfront with anybody in several years. She found that it was a little unnerving to open up the past she had been trying so hard to forget. "Actually, I went through it myself. I'm a widow."

CHAPTER NINE

Jackson stared at Nina. She was so young, maybe thirty-two, or somewhere near that. Awful young to be a widow. He really was at a loss suddenly on what to say. So he said the obvious. "I'm sorry for your loss. At your age, at any age, that's a horrible blow."

Her gaze flickered, and he wasn't sure what he saw in those hazel eyes of hers. Was that uncertainty or weariness…

"I don't really talk about it much. And I can't speak to exactly what your mother is going through, because I wasn't married nearly as long as your mom. If they'd been married since she was nineteen, that's a long time to spend with your soulmate and then to lose them. I had only been married about two years. But yes, it's hard no matter the timeline."

Her words rang somewhat empty. He tried to figure out what wasn't hitting right and then he was ashamed he was even thinking it. She was a widow. *What was there to not feel right about, and who was he to judge anyway?* He was sorry for her. Here he had reached the ripe old age of thirty-five and found no one to love him. She had already lost the person she loved.

"I'm thinking, even before you told me your story, that my mom being here next to you is a good thing." He paused at a table with a lot of old camping equipment on it. He fingered a gray speckled coffee kettle. It was mostly just for distraction. He looked at her. "My dad was a big guy in personality, stature, and ideas. He was just big. He could dominate, not in a bad way, but everything about him was so high energy, that others could kind of get lost in his shadow. My mom is feisty normally and could hold her own with him, but she's lost her fire. She's seemed to sparkle again lately. Does that make sense?"

She smiled, and he liked that smile.

"Yes, you're making sense. She's been grieving and is finding her way. You should have seen her haggling over the price of this overpriced piece of furniture. She was not going to let the guy take advantage of her. You could tell he enjoyed the haggling, too. It was fun watching them come to an agreement on a price, but it took me by surprise. I guess I thought," her nose crinkled up, "I guess I thought that because of who you are, she would just shell out the money and be done. But she didn't, and she really had fun doing it. And the guy got a fair price. He was very happy. That's just how these flea markets are, you know. Unless they really need to sell something, they're not going to sell it real cheap. But if they've got something good, they are willing to haggle. And this is a great piece of furniture. I enjoyed watching her. I learned a few things because actually I'm not very good at haggling. They can take me to the cleaners nearly every time."

He chuckled. "Well, that sounds like my mom. If you get taken to the cleaners all the time, then why do you come here?"

She smiled again, and his gut tightened. "Because it's just fun to watch people who know what they're doing get really good deals."

"I guess so. But, anyway, thanks for bringing my mom here today."

"You're welcome. And there's the piece of furniture right there. See, isn't it beautiful?"

He looked over a few feet away from them where she was pointing and saw a Pepto-Bismol pink cabinet and almost tripped over his own feet. "My mother bought *that?*"

Nina threw her head back and laughed. "Yes, she did, and it will look beautiful in that main room. It's perfect for that beach house or a beach house inn. She's got a vision for the inn, and this is an inspiration piece. So is the other one."

He frowned. "Depends on what it's inspiring." He looked at the other armoire beside it. Thankfully, it was white and had been scraped on the edges but it was nowhere near atrocious as the pink thing. "Well, at least it's not pink." He chuckled and she smiled.

"You better get ready because she might buy more pink items if she sees them. She really likes pink."

"I don't know who this woman is, but I've never seen a pink item anywhere in our house at the ranch."

Looking at the atrocious pink thing, he was about to reconsider the thought his mom was doing good, making progress. The awful pink thing made him wonder whether she might actually be losing her mind. It was awful and that was all there was to it. He laughed. "Do you like that terrible piece of furniture?"

"I think it's pretty. In the right environment, it will make a fun statement. And if it's sanded some, along the edges to let the wood peek through, it will give it more character. Personally, I'm looking forward to seeing what your mother does."

"It's just nothing like anything she's ever decorated with before."

Nina looked thoughtful. After a moment, she ventured, "Have you ever thought that somewhere along the way before you boys came along, she altered her taste to match more of what your dad would like?"

"Maybe. Dad was very opinionated, he knew what he wanted and just kind of swept others along with his plans. But he would never have made Mom make choices she didn't want to make."

"Maybe so. I'm not saying he would or did. I'm just saying maybe she wanted to make him happy. And then you boys came along and no girls, and there was obviously no love for pink anywhere in her life."

Was that true? His mother had great taste; at least, that was what everyone said. He was a guy—what did he know? But *pink*? He could not wrap his head around it.

"You know, it's not the end of the world. And it made your mother so happy. Believe me, her eyes lit up."

And that was the thing that let him know that no matter how much he hated the pink thing, he would grin and bear it. Because he wanted his mother to light up again. He wanted this sedate, elegant woman who was a shell of the mother he'd had before his father died to light up and become the woman she used to be. A happy, engaging woman who smiled often and was full of life. He wanted it as much for him and his brothers as he did for her.

And he knew it was what his father would want too.

* * *

"You should have seen his expression when he first saw the pink armoire." Nina chuckled as she sipped her coffee the next morning.

"I can only imagine the shocked look." Alice had invited Nina to come over for coffee with her this morning after Jackson and Nina had brought the furniture home last night. She wanted Nina's opinion on room colors because she was an artist, and now that she'd hired Seth, she was ready to get serious. They had just settled into their chairs. Alice was secretly wanting to gauge how things had gone between Nina and Jackson. He had teased her about the armoire after he'd used a dolly to get it into the house. And he'd seemed at ease with Nina.

"You should have been there. Alice, it was adorable. I held my laughter in, but thoroughly enjoyed the experience. I think seeing the white armoire and knowing you had also bought it helped him believe you haven't lost all your sanity."

"Men are most comfortable in a world of tans, browns, rusts, and black. Over time, I decorated with colors of their world and loved making them comfortable all these years. But I loved that pink armoire the instant I saw it and knew this time I was decorating in tones that make me happy. I need that right now and I plan to tone it down with some whitewash. It will be fabulous. I wanted to thank you for going with Jackson yesterday. I sprang that on you, but I hope you had a good time."

"I did. Jackson is a great guy."

"I think so. He has a lot on his shoulders. I worry about him and think he needs to relax. He works too much since he's taken on the responsibilities of his dad. During the accident, when William rode into the river and was caught by something beneath the recently flooded river, Jackson was riding closest to his dad. He has always felt that he didn't do enough to save William." She saw shock on Nina's face.

"Really? Why would he feel responsible?"

"Because my husband drowned in the river when they were doing a roundup. He took his horse into the river to cross it, and it swept him off the back of the horse and pulled him under. Jackson was right behind him, and he couldn't get to his dad. He hasn't forgiven himself."

Nina gasped. "That would be a hard thing to get over. To be close but unable to get to the one you loved? Horrible."

Alice nodded. "Yes. It's more than someone should have to bear, but it's my Jackson's cross to bear. I haven't been able to make him understand that it wasn't his fault. I finally figured out, in the end, we all have to travel our own journey."

"Yes, that statement is so true."

Later, after Nina went back home, Alice sat down to make a list. She needed to make some contacts and find a housekeeper and an excellent chef for the inn. That was a priority if she was going to make a success of the place. She would be the hostess, but she couldn't do it all. She was having so much fun getting the inn ready to open. Now that she'd hired Seth Roark to start renovating, she felt a sense of purpose. Seth seemed perfect for the job and his ideas were good. And he seemed as excited about the renovation as she was. And that meant a lot to her. She was counting the days until he would begin work.

She was also going to have to decide on which of Nina's paintings she was going to feature in the bedrooms. She was thinking of giving each room a theme; Nina had enough paintings that she could do this. Her paintings were marvelous. There were brightly colored seascapes, sunsets, and sunrises. They would brighten up the rooms. She was really surprised that Nina didn't have her paintings in galleries, they were so excellent. But she didn't even sign them and there was a room full of them. It had been startling to walk into the room so full of the beauty of Nina's canvases and the enormity of her talent. Alice planned to make it a point to get some attention for the art, and she had no doubt Nina would be autographing the paintings and selling them soon.

Nina was a mystery in very many ways. She was a young widow, but she said very little about her husband or of her life before coming to Star Gazer Island. She had an easy way about her and a lot of wisdom for someone so young. Alice already called her a friend and was grateful to have her next door. And she couldn't help but believe she was perfect for Jackson.

She hadn't missed his reaction whenever Nina entered the room, there was an electric charge that she recognized so well—she and William had experienced that young love and attraction when they'd first met...and in the years of their marriage. She told herself not to get too excited about that just because he seemed to perk up around her neighbor; that in no way meant anything about love. Jackson was a tough nut to crack. And she knew pushing him too much would backfire on her. So now that she'd introduced them, she had backed off and would let them navigate their attraction on their own. At least for now.

She had the inn to worry about. Her friends had

been calling, curious whether the rumors they had heard were true. She hadn't been sure how her friends would react to her becoming an innkeeper. Oh, an inn owner—she was sure they would think it was a fun investment for her. But to be the innkeeper…they hadn't been very receptive. Why was she going to spend her time renting rooms out to people, feeding them and cleaning up after them? That had been the overall gist of their reactions. They had been sympathetic, though, believing she was going through a phase. Some suggested she needed to see a grief counselor. She did not need to see a grief counselor. She had grieved. Was grieving and would continue to grieve William. But she had to do this, was driven to do this new beginning.

But she needed to hire some help.

Her phone rang, and she recognized her friend Lisa Blair's number. Lisa had been traveling and they'd ended up playing phone tag, their calls always missing. She smiled as she answered and she prepared herself for the same reception that all of her other friends had given her when she'd told them the news.

"Lisa, it's so good to hear from you. Are you back in town?"

"I am, and I have heard some exciting news about you. Is it true? Are you actually renovating that quaint old inn at Star Gazer Island?"

Alice's pulse picked up at hearing excitement in Lisa's voice. "I am. So you don't think I'm as off my rocker as everyone else believes?"

"No, I don't. I'm thrilled about it. I think it's a wonderful idea. And it'll get you away from that ranch where you've been hibernating. This is a fantastic idea and will be good for you. I'm a little jealous."

Alice heard the sincerity in Lisa's words, and it warmed her heart. Lisa had been through a terrible divorce two years ago after her lawyer husband left her for a younger woman with whom he'd already had a child. He'd had a second family on the side and the baby was now about a year old. He and Lisa had never been able to have children, so this had made his betrayal even more hurtful. Lisa had been traveling the world and spending the money that she had gotten in the settlement. And though she'd seemed to have been having the time of her life, Alice had often wondered whether she was as happy as she wanted everyone to believe. Now she thought she heard a hint of longing in Lisa's voice.

"Lisa, I would love for you to come see what I'm doing. Give me some of your excellent advice. We can talk."

"That sounds fun. I'm actually driving over Harbor Bridge. I can swing over your way now, if that works for you."

"It's perfect." Excitement bubbled inside Alice as she rattled off the address. After she'd set the phone down, she was smiling.

Fifteen minutes later, Lisa's sporty Jaguar whipped into the drive. Lisa was a dark brunette with russet highlights. She was tall and had a full figure and an energetic personality.

The minute she saw Lisa she hurried down the steps to greet her with a hug. "I'm so glad to see you. It's been too long. And thank you for not telling me I had lost my mind."

"You haven't lost your mind." Arms linked, they turned to look at the inn. "I have always loved this place. There is a sense of peace that surrounds it. And many amazing dishes have been served on that gorgeous veranda with the sun setting on the horizon. I can't wait to see that again. I can't wait to see inside and hear your plans."

"Then let's go." Arm in arm, they walked to the front porch and up the steps. Alice opened the door and waved Lisa inside first.

Lisa gasped. "Oh, my goodness, I can feel it. There's happiness in this house. Oh, Alice, I am so very jealous. What a treasure. This is a brilliant inspiration to reopen the pretty lady." Her friend looked at her with awe in her eyes.

"I met William here when I was working my first

summer of college. And after he died, I kept being drawn to this beach to walk along it and I cried buckets of tears. And one day, I stopped to look at the inn...I always loved it. We came here several times through the years before it closed, and I just have such wonderful memories. And you'll think I'm crazy or sentimental, but it called to me. And I knew this was what I wanted to do. I've felt energized and inspired ever since I made the decision. Thank goodness my boys are trying so hard to understand and be supportive. And it's a short and easy trip here from the ranch, so I'm not worrying them too much. But I had to do it."

Lisa nodded. "It's so nice that you have them to be supportive."

Alice knew that Lisa had no family to support her, and she suddenly felt bad that she might not have been there for her friend through her divorce like she should have been.

They had walked down the long hallway and were now in the kitchen area overlooking the water. Alice paused beside the large island. "How are you doing?"

Lisa went to the windows and took in the view. "I'm doing fine. You know me—have suitcase, can travel."

"And like I said, how are you?"

Lisa turned to look at her and she glimpsed

sadness in her friend's eyes. "I'm struggling. At first, the traveling helped me get away. When I was traveling, I was able to outrun the nastiness of my imploding life. I gave it a good try though and it was better than staying here. I couldn't stay here and hear about Mason and his new fiancée and the baby. I had too much anger inside and I didn't like the person I was becoming."

"I'm so sorry that happened to you. Finding out your husband had a second family has to be terribly hard. It would be unimaginable, actually."

"It was. The feelings of betrayal. I felt like such a fool. I'm so very sorry you lost your William. And he would be so proud of you right now, he adored you, everyone knew it. As for me, I'm trying to overcome the angry person who has taken over my spirit. And I didn't mean to have a pity party just now. What I meant was, traveling helped me at first. And I even dated some in France, but it didn't last—was actually a disaster but I am not going to talk about that. I just wasn't ready for it to last. And now, the traveling has gotten old. That's what I meant about me struggling. I'm rambling and like my ramblings, I'm just not sure where to go from here."

Alice felt deep empathy for her vibrant friend. "I'm confident that you'll figure it out. Come on, let me show you the inn. The renovations start in a few days and I can hardly wait." Alice took her on a tour of the house and her mind was working rapidly as in each room Lisa just came alive and was so encouraging.

"It will be amazing. I can see it now," Alice said as they walked back into the kitchen.

Alice pulled a pitcher of iced raspberry tea from the refrigerator and poured them both a glass. They walked out to the patio near the beach and sank into cushioned chairs overlooking the ocean.

"Lisa, I have an idea. I'm just going to throw it out here and all you can do is say no. But, I'm looking for a chef. I know you are an amazing cook. Didn't you go to culinary school before you married Mason?"

"I did but I didn't finish because I met Mason and married him. I have to admit, though, it always came in handy when we threw parties for his clients and partners."

"Your parties are legendary. You're very talented. So, what do you think?" Alice watched Lisa expectantly. Lisa's eyes clouded with what she thought was confusion. And then Alice realized maybe she hadn't made herself clear. "Lisa, I'm asking you if you would come to work for me. I'm believing and having faith that the inn is going to be a huge success with the right people beside me. And with your amazing dishes, I believe you would be key in making my dream a reality. I understand completely if you aren't interested—"

Lisa's eyes suddenly started sparkling. "Yes. I would love to do this. Are you absolutely sure, though?"

This felt right. So right. "Absolutely."

Lisa took a sip of the tea, then smiled. "It sounds like a great adventure. When I went to culinary school, I had visions of opening a restaurant."

"And now you shall. I'm thinking that once we get the inn open, we can offer a wedding venue too. There're all kinds of options that we could do."

Lisa smiled brightly. "I'm in."

"Wonderful. I'm so excited. We have a lot to discuss." She couldn't believe that Lisa would want to do something like this. But she did look happy. "We're going to be amazing." She held up her glass of tea.

Lisa lifted hers and the two glasses clinked in a toast. "Amazing. To new adventures. This is going to be fun."

CHAPTER TEN

"Tucker, swing over behind that one and bring him this way." Jackson stood by the gate and waited as Tucker rode his horse over and cut the calf out of the group. It dodged Tucker's horse and raced toward the gate Jackson was holding open and into the pen next door. He shut the gate. "Thanks. That does it. I think we've got them all."

The herd had been ornery this morning so it was a relief to finish.

"I went by Mom's yesterday," Tucker said. "The place is looking great. And she seems happier." He rubbed his jaw. "Like she's got something to look forward to."

Jackson bent down and scrubbed Shep behind the

ears. Socks rushed over for a head rub, not wanting Shep to get more attention than he did. He gave them both a good rub. They helped round up the cattle and had done an excellent job today, as usual. It had been a week since he'd been to his mother's and he and Nina had picked up the pink monstrosity. Nina had been on his mind all week. "Yeah, I'm thinking the same thing. If it doesn't end up being too much work for her."

"She's been busy this week. Hired the contractor and you know her friend Lisa? Did you know Mom hired her to be the chef for the inn?"

Jackson was startled but interested. "Last I heard, wasn't she traveling around the world or something?"

"I think she was just getting her lousy ex-husband back for gallivanting in another way. But yeah, I think she's been traveling a lot. She seemed like she was excited. They had been working on menus when I was there. And she had baked some croissants or something with some French cream inside them that was delicious. I know if she's going to be there cooking, I may go by more. The woman's cooking is amazing. The place could be a success with just the food that Lisa prepares. She has a knack, I think. Mom says she thinks she was just getting bored traveling."

Jackson thought his mother had made a good choice. "Lisa seems like a great gal. She's always been a good friend of Mom's, so I hope it works out great for them."

"Me too. I also met her neighbor, Nina. She's pretty. Though she's not real talkative."

"She talked to me. She seems great."

Tucker hitched a brow. "Interesting, you must have made an impression because she mentioned you."

Jackson looked up from petting Shep. "She did? Why?"

"I don't know. She just asked if you were working hard."

Jackson liked that she'd asked about him. He had been really busy. It was the end of the quarter and taxes were due, and they had the big sale coming up and he had to get everything in order for that. Everything together had meant late nights at the computer and days here working with his brothers. He'd been totally avoiding her.

Why? Because something about her captivated him. He was interested in her and he knew his mother was hoping there was something there between them. But he'd realized it was problematic. Nina was his mother's new neighbor, her friend. They lived right next door to each other. What if this interest in Nina was short-lived? What if they went out, and realized there wasn't anything there? What if they went out and thought something was there and then they split? Nina would still be his mother's neighbor, her friend, and it could be awkward.

"Mom said that you took her to the flea market and picked up that pink thing that's in her living room now." Tucker gave a rough laugh. "That *thing* sitting in the corner of the living room space made me think of Pepto-Bismol. It's awful."

They both laughed.

Jackson shook his head. "You should have seen my reaction when Nina pointed it out to me. That's what we had driven into town to pick up. I had almost passed out. Nina didn't let me live it down the rest of the day."

"That may be why she was asking about your work schedule—she was thinking you were avoiding her."

"Maybe so. But she's nice. She's a good neighbor for Mom. And even though there's an age difference, they seem to get along well. And sadly, she's also a widow."

Tucker laid his hands across his saddle horn and looked at him with narrowed eyes. "Really, at her age? That's a shame." He paused then shook his head. "It's a shame at any age. I didn't mean it that way. It's been terrible for Mom too."

Jackson stood. "I know what you mean. Nina is young and she's been through a lot, I think. And Lisa has been through a lot, too. Maybe the three of them

111

can be a support for each other."

"Yeah, maybe so. That would be good." Tucker tipped his hat back and stared up at the sun. "Man, it's a hot one. I'm off for a shower and meeting Riley at the pool hall. Want to come?"

"No, I've got some computer work to get through. Have fun."

Tucker scoffed. "I'm going to win some money off our brother. I'm going to have a good time."

Jackson laughed. "Take it easy on our little brother."

"Hey, he beat me last time, so fair is fair."

Jackson watched him ride toward the barn. Then he headed across the lot toward the house. He still had Nina on his mind and by the time he reached the house, Jackson decided to call her. He went into the kitchen, poured himself a glass of cold iced tea and headed into the den. He sat down on the leather sofa and propped his boots on the coffee table. He pulled his phone out of the clip on his belt, scrolled through his contacts and after a brief hesitation called Nina's number. His pulse increased as the phone rang. He should have taken a shower before calling but once he decided to call her, he didn't want to wait.

"Jackson, is everything okay?"

He smiled at the sound of her voice and he was glad he'd called but realized he had worried her. "Hi,

Nina. Everything is fine. Mom is fine. How are you?"

"Oh, seeing your name on my screen worried me. I'm glad Alice is okay. I'm fine. How are you?"

He tried to relax and settled into the couch. "I've been busy, getting things lined up for a big upcoming cattle sale we have each year. It takes a lot of organization. How are you?" Why had he asked that question again? Nerves. He wasn't used to nerves, and they felt weird.

She gave a small laugh, as if realizing by his repetition that he might be nervous. "I'm fine," she said slowly as if teasing him and making sure he understood that she was indeed fine. He smiled as she continued, "I'm having a glass of wine on the porch right now. I've been painting all day and I love the picture so I'm celebrating."

"Sounds like it must be a beautiful painting. What's it of?"

"The inn. I've been spending some time next door with your mother and Lisa. I really like her and think they're going to be fantastic together with the inn and the guests. They're having a great time with ideas. And I had the idea to do a painting of the inn at sunset as a gift for your mom. I think she's going to love it."

Her kindness hit him. Nina had been nothing but helpful to his mother since she'd bought the inn. "That's very nice, very generous of you. Nina, I just want to thank you for being so helpful to my mother."

Nina laughed softly and he loved the sound. "I'm just being a good neighbor. Besides, I really like Alice. And she's been just as kind to me. We're friends."

"I'm glad. I think you must have needed a good neighbor, being isolated on that end of the peninsula."

"Yes, I can't deny that. But I'm so grateful your mother bought the inn. It's going to be lovely. It could have just as easily been bought by someone who wanted to turn it into a party destination with a lot of loud music and late nights."

He laughed. "I hadn't thought of that. I see your point now."

She chuckled. "Did you know the new contractor starts tomorrow? Alice is very excited."

"I'm glad. I checked him out and he's a good guy. Has a stellar reputation and does great work. She made a good choice."

"I think so. She's one smart cookie. Which she showed again by hiring Lisa as the chef."

"I heard the news, and yeah, Lisa's parties are legendary because of how fantastic her food is. Tucker told me. I've been busy and haven't made it in to see her this week."

"I thought the pink armoire ran you off."

He heard the smile in her voice and smiled too. "It almost did. Hey," he plunged forward, "I'm calling to see if you might want to come out to the ranch tomorrow and go riding. I could show you some of the landscapes you might want to paint."

There was a distinct pause and he wondered whether she was going to turn him down. After all, he'd gotten her number as an emergency precaution, not as a potential date.

"I'd like that. If you're sure you have the time to show me."

"I have it. I'm all caught up. I'll text you the directions. How does ten o'clock sound?"

"Perfect."

He was still smiling a few minutes later when they ended the call. He had a date with Nina. It felt special. As if he stood on the edge of something big.

Something meaningful.

CHAPTER ELEVEN

Alice stood in the kitchen, lost in thought, staring through the French door out toward the sea. She had so much on her mind: paint colors, room themes, menu choices, to name a few things. And yet here she stood, doing nothing.

Lisa came in through the side door that opened to the driveway. Several grocery bags dangled from her fingers. Alice had given her a credit card for the inn so she could pick up any food supplies or utensils she needed in the kitchen to test recipes and all week Lisa had been here working on the menu. Her friend had thrown herself into her new position as the Inn's chef with an excited enthusiasm that Alice was glad to see. Maybe having something positive was exactly what

Lisa needed. A validation of sorts. Seeing her friend's warm smile caused Alice's funky mood to brighten instantly.

"Good morning. Can I help you carry anything?"

"Nope." Lisa gently kicked the door shut with her foot, then stood there holding the sacks, grinning at her. "I've got it. I couldn't help myself. I wanted to test some more ideas. I know we have a few months until we're ready to open, but I want to pick exactly the right dishes, so it could take time. We want our signature items to set the tone for the menu, and there are so many things to decide. A signature dessert is a must if we want to do this right." She set the sacks on the counter. "And going to the store is a chore. Hey, I'm a poet and didn't even know it."

"You always make me laugh. I've been pinching myself all week to remind me that I didn't dream it and that you are actually coming on this journey with me."

Lisa put her fisted hands on her hips and gave her a frank look. "I'm so glad you invited me along. Alice, really, you have no idea how much I needed the challenge of this job. Desperately. I was wandering all over the world, but really I've been lost at sea."

"I think we've both been lost at sea." Alice reached to unload a bag. "Let's put this stuff in the refrigerator and then kick off our shoes and take a walk on the beach. We can grab something to drink and stroll and brainstorm ideas or we can just talk. I've missed you. Our few phone calls while you were gone just weren't enough."

"I think that's a brilliant idea." She started unloading a bag. "I'll put this stuff up while you get us something to sip on, and then let's hit that sand as quick as possible."

Moments later, barefoot, each carrying a metal bottle full of savory iced raspberry tea, they were walking along the beach side by side.

Lisa looked at her and paused "Now, tell me how you're doing. You looked sad when I came in this morning."

Alice reached down and picked up a pebble. She rubbed her finger across it before she tossed it out into the water, watching it as it plopped into a wave and was swallowed up by the tide. "I used to toss those in the water and make wishes." She shot Lisa a rueful glance. "Not anymore. Instead, I feel like that pebble. I feel like I'm sinking much of the time. Some days I think I'm doing okay, making progress and other days I'm desolate. I still cry like a baby sometimes. And I sound like I haven't made any progress, but I have. I really have. However, today is one of those days that making myself care about anything has been hard. I needed this walk."

The wind whipped Lisa's shoulder-length hair

about like feathers. She pushed it behind her ears as she studied Alice. "I can't imagine how hard William's death has been on you. You have every right to mourn as long as you need to. You have every right to be angry that your sweetie was stolen from you like he was, dying so young—and yes, sixty-one was young. We are still young. But I've learned life can change in an instant. To be blunt, I couldn't imagine two years ago that I'd be standing here with you and that you would be a widow now or that I'd be a divorced, jilted woman. Two years ago, you had it all, and I thought I did too. I thought my marriage was great. Perfect. Oh, so lovely. Ha, little did I know it was about to implode and I'd be dreaming of strangling the love of my life in his sleep. Middle-aged crazy is just crazy. Life is so full of unexpected junk; it's hard."

"I'm so sorry, Lisa." She felt for her friend and could understand her angry outburst. Lisa had been so in love with her husband, Mason. Crazy about him had been more like it, and everyone knew it. Like she had been about William. When the news circulated that Mason had another family on the side, a mistress and a baby, it had been a huge blow to Lisa. To everyone. Alice couldn't imagine how Lisa had felt about the betrayal. It had been a few months before William's accident and both events showed how quickly life could change. William and all of their circle of friends

119

had been just as shocked as Lisa. William had always been a wonderful judge of character and yet, he'd never suspected Mason of such an outrageous affair.

"Lisa, you've handled the betrayal and divorce. I'm afraid with William's death happening so soon after you found out about Mason, that I was in my own world while you went through the divorce. But I'd hoped staying busy like you were doing was good for you. Now, I'm wondering if maybe you needed a place to rest. A place to stop running and maybe find peace with all of it. Like I'm trying to do. Find peace and move forward."

"I wasn't ready at first. Just needed to run away as far as I could get. But it caught up to me."

As if in mutual agreement, they started walking again. It felt good to move, as if walking and moving forward on the beach was the same as moving forward in their lives.

"Do you know, Alice, we're both starting new beginnings? The truth is, it's scary. And me running around like that was just because I didn't have the courage to face what I needed to face. I was just running from one beautiful place to another, spending time on this beach and that beach and this ski resort and that ski resort. It might have looked like on my social media like I was happy all the time but it's an illusion. Most horrifying to me is that I still want him sometimes."

Alice felt a stab of horror for her friend. What a terrible situation to be in. Love didn't always end at betrayal. Just like love didn't always end at death. Her heart ached with love gone too soon. "I'm so sorry, Lisa."

"Me too. The fact that after all he's done to me, and everything he continues to do, I can't understand why I have these feelings that well up inside of me sometimes. It makes me feel desperate. It's so aggravating. Honestly, it makes me so angry, you know? That he would toss away the life we'd built and that I believed was perfect and then act as if I'm a bug he wants to keep grinding into the pavement with his shoe. I just don't understand the man that has taken the place of the man I thought I knew."

"Your anger and perplexity are completely understandable." She knew about anger. "I have felt anger too. Anger at William for riding his horse into that river. He knew better than to do that. He *knew* how treacherous flash floods are and he *knew* that after a river has flooded and the water seems calm again that there is no telling what might be hiding beneath that water's surface. He'd witnessed barbed wire and trees in the water after a flood. He knew of the dangerous things that could be there to harm anyone who ventured into the water too soon. And yet, he tried to cross the river anyway." Tears stung her eyes.

They stared at each other, and Alice saw the shimmer of tears matching her own eyes in her friend's eyes.

Lisa swallowed, then gave a light, sardonic laugh. "I think anger is part of the recovery. So maybe that's a good sign."

Alice inhaled a deep breath of fresh air. "Maybe so." She turned to look back down the beach at the inn in the distance, with the bright-blue sky and white clouds as a backdrop. It was charming and lightened her heart just looking at it.

Lisa turned to look too. "That old inn has weathered a lot of storms and has survived. It gives me hope. And makes me happy just looking at it."

Alice inhaled the fresh air again then exhaled, letting the emotions that had been tugging at her dissipate. "Exactly what I was thinking. I believe the inn represents a new beginning for us. I did a lot of walking and mourning on this strip of beach. And that day I was walking here like I had so many times over the last year, it was as if it called to me. Like it had been sitting here for five years, waiting for me to open it back up."

"Waiting for you to buy it," Lisa said. "And to bring us both back to life here."

"Yes, exactly. I'd been ignoring it, and that day, it

just grabbed my heart and I couldn't stop myself. I took that picture of that For Sale sign and I called Burt right then and swore him to secrecy. I had to because I couldn't have him telling my boys at that time. I couldn't have him break the surprise to them. I knew it was going to blindside them and they were quite shocked, and I didn't want it coming from anybody but me. But I also didn't want them stopping me, so we bought it out of secrecy and then I broke the news to them."

"And it looks like they're handling it. They're just worried about their mama."

"Yes, they are. But I worry about them too. Just like I worry about you. But you know, all I can think of is that we're all moving forward in our own way. And we'll all get through this. You will too. The boys know that William would be the first one telling us all to get ourselves in gear. He'd tell us to go out and win at life. He always said that." Thinking of his booming voice saying exactly that caused a smile to bloom across her face and in her heart. "That big giant of a man would wag a finger at me or the boys when he'd say it. Now, some days remembering him wagging that finger at me is the only thing keeping me going."

"I envy you. Not William's death, but I envy you knowing that for a while you really had it all. Alice, he did love you so much. He didn't choose to leave you, and that has to be a great comfort. Your life wasn't an illusion. It was a shining example to all of us. And I'm so glad for that."

On impulse, Alice threw her arms around Lisa and hugged her. It was so true; her sweet William had left her not because he wanted to, but because it was his time. But Lisa's jerk husband had betrayed her, betrayed everything that Lisa and his vows had stood for. "One day, I hope you have the courage to start over with someone new. That you can trust again and know what it feels like to be cherished."

Lisa sniffed and her arms tightened around Alice before she pulled back. "I don't think I can ever commit again. The betrayal is just too raw, even after two years. I might be a fool once, but only once. This girl is never saying vows again. I can appreciate a good-looking man, but that's it. Now, enough wallowing. I feel the need to bake. Let's get back to the inn and start working out our menu. A little taste testing is exactly what we need."

Alice had felt that sense of off, moody feeling earlier, but now she felt better. This talk had reminded her where she'd been, what she'd had and to never take it for granted. And to always remember that once she'd had it all. She'd been blessed and she knew it. She could do this. It was what William would want. And it was what she wanted.

Arm in arm, drinking their sweet tea, they strolled back up the beach. The beach had grown busier as they'd been walking, and they passed several people walking and they said hello as they passed them. A tiny woman in a big red hat walked along, looking for shells. When they passed, she looked up, revealing startling blue eyes in a very weathered face. She immediately went back to looking for shells and didn't say hello when they called hello. Alice had seen her a few times, and she never spoke. Alice didn't press her; people had the right to talk or not to talk. But she was curious about the woman and planned to find out her name. She seemed lonely, and a couple of times Alice saw her pass the inn and stare at it. She wondered why. Maybe she just loved the inn like Alice did.

As they walked through the gate into the garden area, Alice stopped and looked about. "We should plan on a gazebo or a pavilion and more flagstone. I'm seeing weddings in the inn's future. What do you think?"

Lisa beamed. "As long as you're not seeing my wedding in its future, then I think it's a fantastic idea. This inn was meant for weddings. And I love to cook fancy food. I think we have us a winning combination."

Alice did too.

CHAPTER TWELVE

Standing beside the stable with Shep and Socks watching him from the shade, flat on their bellies with their jaws resting on their outstretched paws, Jackson waited for Nina. He liked Nina. This lovely neighbor was a complete surprise that had come from this move his mother had made. And because she was such a good neighbor and new friend to his mother, he couldn't mess this up.

He liked the fact that Nina, though a little over twenty years younger than his mother, seemed very comfortable around his mom. And yet she had moments when she seemed very uncomfortable around him. It was an off-balanced mixture, and he wanted to find out why.

WHAT NEW BEGINNINGS ARE MADE OF

"We're just going riding," he said, glancing at his dogs as if they were interested in his love life.

Right. He had been having thoughts about his future lately—whether it was because his mother had made such a huge change in her life and mentioned part of that was there were no grandchildren yet, or that he had met Nina and felt drawn to her like no other woman he'd ever been around. He wasn't sure what brought it on, but he was certain that he was powerfully attracted to Nina.

The facts were, he was thirty-five years old, and it was time for him to start thinking about his future. Past time.

His thoughts continued to churn as he watched Nina drive down the ranch lane. He wondered whether Nina could be the one who could change his life.

His blood pressure spiked, waiting. He smiled and felt excited about the day as he opened the car door for her. When she looked up at him and smiled before stepping out of the car, he knew he'd never anticipated time spent with a woman more than this moment. Her thick hair was pulled back in a ponytail. She wore jeans and running shoes and a short-sleeve blouse that would keep her cool in the breeze on a sunny day like today.

"Did you make it here without any problems?"

Her smile turned teasing. "GPS brought me right

to the gate." And thankfully nobody ran out in front of me."

He felt like a goofy kid as he chuckled. "That's a good thing."

Socks and Shep had followed him out to the car and she smiled beautifully down at them.

"You guys must be Jackson's working dogs. I've heard good things about you." She bent down to the smiling, wiggling masses of excited fur and petted them enthusiastically.

He laughed at their antics while he felt really jealous of the way she was rubbing them down. "That's them. And if you keep that up, they're going to load up with you and leave me."

She laughed and turned her face to beam at him. "You would miss them, wouldn't you?"

"I would. This week, they were indispensable when we were herding cattle." He couldn't help teasing her and her eyes narrowed at him. "Okay, yes, I would miss them. They are great dogs and they listen to me air my troubles without judging me."

"See, you're very good doggies. I told him so," she said to the eager dogs and gave them each a last petting, then straightened. "Dogs are excellent listeners. I'm finding I talk to Buttercup all the time now. I'm not sure what I ever did without her."

He wondered, not for the first time, whether she

had been lonely living there at the end of the island. "I thought you were going to bring her out today."

"Actually, she stayed with your mother and Lisa. They are working on recipes today and insisted I leave her with them. Your mom was worried that the ride out would be too much for her."

"She might have been right. These fellas are used to the conditions out here, but Buttercup is an inside dog and might overheat. So Mom to the rescue." He smiled. "So, you ready to ride then?"

She heaved in a big breath and then expelled it slowly as he closed the door and they walked toward the barns. "I've been gearing myself up for it. It's been a long time. But I am excited, just feeling a little angst. I almost tried to talk myself out of it last night. But your mom dropped by to watch the sunset with me, and I happened to mention it. She was so excited and told me you were a fantastic rider and that you would keep me safe. And that I would have a wonderful time, and that's when she talked me into leaving Buttercup with her. She adores you, in case you didn't know."

He chuckled again, this time a bit embarrassed, knowing full well that his mother could be zealous in her praise of him and his brothers. "The feeling is mutual. She's a great horsewoman herself, not that she's ridden in years. But she used to love it."

"People's interests change. She said there was

some spectacular plots of land here and even suggested that there were some places that would be beautiful to paint. Like you suggested."

He liked that idea. "One of the places I thought we would ride out to is one of those spots that I'm sure my mom is talking about. With as much land as we have here, the terrain is rugged and there is a lot of scrub brush and a lot of salt grass. We have an array of subject matter for you to paint. In order for you to view some of the most beautiful areas, we'd need to drive the truck, though. With over two hundred thousand acres, it would take a lot more than an afternoon to see it. We'll save the truck tour for another day."

"That sounds great. At the house, I have up mostly seascapes and bright colors, but I do Texas countryside also—I just have this thing for land. I love it and cattle. I'd like to paint some cattle. If you have a place that has cattle and coast, I think that would be a great picture. She told me that your ranch also has a coastline."

"We do. We have some beautiful coastline and we even ferry cattle across the intercoastal canal to the island for grazing. It's beautiful there, a lot like Mustang Beach. It has tons of salt grass. The cattle graze there and it's really nutritious. But that would be a cool picture, I think, with that pretty coastline and then the cattle too. I'm no artist, but I can sure be a tour guide."

She smiled. "Then I think we can safely say that we'll ride a horse today and then when it's convenient for you, I would love for you to take me out to these cows that graze on an island."

"That can be arranged." He liked this more and more, knowing this wasn't the only day he had to spend with her.

She walked with him to the barn, where he had two horses waiting, tied to the fence. He had his gelding and a mare that had a great temperament and would be a safe ride. He wasn't taking any chances on something happening to Nina.

"There are some facilities in the office there in the barn if you need them before we ride. We'll be roughing it some but there is a small camp cabin Mom had built a few years back near where we're going, so you won't have to be completely left to the mercy of the bushes."

She laughed loudly at that. "Too funny. I think I'll go check out the facilities, as you call them. It sounds like I may be in for a long day."

"It's the cowboy way, but Mom didn't like roughing it that much and so had little overnight cabins built in some areas that she enjoyed. This is one of those."

"I'll have to thank her later."

While he waited on her to return, Jackson untied the reins and then, when she came back outside, he held the saddle horn with one hand and offered her his other hand. "Ready?"

"As I'll ever be." She grabbed the saddle; he moved his hand, and she was able to grab a part of the saddle and hoist herself up. Halfway up she wobbled, and Jackson placed his hand on her thigh to steady her.

"Hang on there," he said.

She glanced down at him. "Thanks. Just call me graceful. I might have fallen backward."

He smiled. "Not with me standing here. If you'd fallen, I would've caught you."

She put her leg over the horse and slid into the saddle.

He patted the top of her thigh and then pulled his hand away, not wanting her to think he was getting too friendly. He needed to bide his time, but the truth was he was hoping to soon be friendly enough to kiss Nina Hanson. "There you go, leg over and settle in."

"Thank you." She settled into the saddle, looking a bit wary.

"I'll saddle up. You're okay. Hilde is a good horse."

He moved to his horse. Better there than standing beside her, looking up at her. In a second, he was in the saddle and then they were walking their horses out, down the lane toward the entrance to the pasture they would cross on the way to the creeks and the swimming hole he and his brothers used growing up. He knew this was probably one place that his mother had been thinking about because it was beautiful and at sunset, the way that sun hit on the water, it couldn't be beaten. It was almost as beautiful as the coastline at sunset. It was one of the McIntyre Ranch's little bits of heaven.

"You ride pretty good. I would never guess you haven't ridden in however long you said it was."

"Well, I'm thrilled to just be in the saddle. I figure anything other than falling off is a plus."

"To be honest, I thought maybe—I don't know why I thought it—but maybe that the horse might intimidate you. But you seem to be fine. But I gave you Hilde there because Hilde is a good gal. She's easygoing, and she loves to take people riding. She's been with us for a long time."

"Well, Hilde is doing a great job making me look good, I think."

"Don't sell yourself short. Anyway, you've got your hands on the reins good. You've got a good seat, sitting in the saddle—you should be comfortable. Now we're not going to go too fast because I don't want to take the chance of you getting bounced off, but we'll work on that."

She eyed him with eyes that at the moment had no wariness in them, and he liked that. Maybe she was getting more comfortable with him.

"You say that like there's going to be more than this trip and the drive to the cows by the sea."

He laughed. "Well, unless you get really perturbed at me and decide you don't like me very much, then I don't see why you can't come out and ride as much as you want, especially since you're going to come out painting. I figure I'll see you when you're painting."

"Right. I forgot that for a few minutes."

She might have forgotten, but he hadn't.

* * *

Nina was going to be sore tomorrow. But she was enjoying herself. And she was more and more comfortable with this calm, sexy cowboy riding beside her. He told her about the birds and the coyotes and wolves that lived on the land, and she could listen to the man talk for hours. It was clear how much he loved this land that had been in their family for so long.

She tried to tamp down the emotions crawling through her like spiders trying to pull her back from—or make her continue—being wary of him. But it was getting harder and harder for her to hear the alarms telling her she couldn't trust her own judgment. The alarms telling her that her emotions were tricking her again.

Was she always going to be satisfied with this quiet life of solitude that she'd made for herself here in South Texas after her terrible relationship disasters? Including her marriage?

She bit her lip as she rode, and as her past rose up to taunt her. It haunted her always, but some days were worse. Her husband, whose increasingly crazy jealousies and the emotional trauma that he'd put her through toward the end of their marriage, had left scars on her emotions. Scars on her psychologically and her belief in her judgment were the leftovers from her marriage that was ending in divorce…when he died in a car accident. She was going to file the next day but then he'd had the crash. Not many people knew this, and she'd lived a lie after his death because everyone believed she was the grieving widow. And she had been sad that he'd died, but there had been no love left at the time of his death.

"You are deep in thought."

His deep voice intruded in her thoughts, and she was grateful to him for that. She smiled and met his inquisitive gaze. "This country is beautiful. I mean, I see it when I'm driving on the roads but being out here riding through it on horseback brings it to life. I like it." And she did, more than she'd thought possible.

His smile warmed. "I'm glad. I love it here, as you can probably tell. It's been in our family since the 1800s. My great-great-granddaddy bought it and settled here. About the same time the King Ranch was being established. They all struck oil around the same time, too. I honestly don't know any other kind of life, nor have I ever thought about any other kind of life."

She smiled at him, enjoying the slow rhythm of the horses as they walked through the pastures. "I don't think I can even imagine you in any other life. I guess I look at you from the moment I ran into you there at the inn as the epitome of a tall, Texas cowboy rancher. I guess that's the way I would always see you."

He cocked his head to the side, and his eyes drilled into her. "Then the question is, does that interest you?"

Butterflies lifted in her stomach and despite all the alarms, she went with her gut. "Yes."

CHAPTER THIRTEEN

A lice was enjoying having Buttercup trot behind her as she moved furniture around in the library room on the first floor. This room didn't need anything but a fresh coat of paint, and she was going to do that while Seth worked on the parts of the inn that needed some construction and especially the bathrooms that would require the most remodeling. Lisa had been by on her way to pick up supplies, and they planned to bake the rest of the afternoon while Seth began working on the renovation. If he planned to work in the kitchen first they'd have to put off baking until he had it finished. But Lisa was so excited about starting to test her menu Alice told her to go ahead and pick up the supplies. Alice was excited too and had begun prepping this room for painting.

The doorbell rang, and her heart skipped. *He was here. The renovations were about to start.* After all this time, her vision, her dream was happening. She started toward the front door but stopped as suddenly unexpected tears sprang to her eyes. Her lip trembled as she tried to hold back the wave of emotions. She tried so hard not to look back…but it was so hard. Moving forward meant distancing herself from William and her life with him. She laid a hand to the library door and took a deep breath. She was expecting her contractor and greeting him with tears streaming down her cheeks was not exactly the best impression.

She hadn't been ambushed by her grief in a while. Oh, a few days ago when she and Lisa had walked on the beach, they'd both gotten emotional but lately she hadn't had the gut-wrenching feeling of loss that could come over unexpectedly.

The doorbell rang again, and she inhaled, wiped her eyes, and moved to glance in the mirror of the first-floor bathroom. She looked a little pale and her eyes a little too bright, but she didn't really look as though she'd been crying.

Hurrying to the front door, she pulled it open. Seth Roark stood on the porch.

"I'm so sorry to keep you waiting. I was in the back. Please come inside." She stepped back, and he came into the foyer.

"Is everything okay?" His pale eyes searched hers.

"Yes, everything is fine. I'm excited to have the renovations starting today. Where are you planning on working first?"

"I'm going to start in the bathrooms here on the first floor. How does that sound?"

"Perfect. When will you do the kitchen? We're going to start working on our menu but we can pause whenever you need us to."

"I'll get the kitchen after I get the bathroom finished. I'm waiting on the stainless steel counters to arrive before I tear the old ones out. That's the plan right now."

She had chosen to go with professional stainless counters and couldn't wait to see the results. "I'm thankful you're going to start the bathroom while you wait. Thank you."

"No need for thanks. That's what you hired me for." He smiled. "I'll get my things and get started tearing out the fixtures. I've called and a renovation dumpster is being delivered. It will be sitting on the driveway for the duration of the renovation."

"Oh, I hadn't thought of that. They're so ugly but a must, so bring it on." She laughed, feeling better as he chuckled with her.

"Yes, they're not the best addition to a nice

landscape but what they represent is a refresh to the house is going on, so think of it that way. And when it's gone the place will be beautiful for your guests."

"Exactly. Well, I'll let you get back to work. My friend, Lisa, who will be the chef here at the inn, is coming by and we'll be doing test baking as we begin to plan the menu for the Star Gazer Inn veranda. I may use you as a tester during the day, if that is okay?"

His smile widened, and the lines around his eyes crinkled, making his blue eyes luminous. "I'll look forward to that perk. Might be the best perk of a job I've ever had because I have a feeling the food will be fantastic."

She felt lighthearted looking at him. "Yes, I'm hoping so. We're going to work very hard to make it special."

"And I'm sure it will be."

Buttercup trotted down the hall to see what was going on and Alice picked her up and held her as Seth headed out to his truck for his supplies. She rubbed Buttercup's fur and watched Seth leave, all broad shouldered and lean hipped. Then she turned and headed to the kitchen, feeling much better than she had just before he'd arrived.

Thirty minutes later, Alice finished preparing the library for painting and planned to tackle it the next day. She was in the kitchen, with the door closed so

Buttercup couldn't get out with Seth coming and going, and she was reading over the recipes they were intended to test today. The kitchen door opened and Lisa walked in, carrying two bags of groceries.

"Hey, I came in the front door since there is a truck blocking the drive and do you know there is a *gorgeous* man in the bathroom?"

Alice chuckled at Lisa's raised brows and words. "Yes, I'm very aware of that. Seth's the contractor I told you was starting today. I didn't see a ring on his finger and I didn't ask if he was married but maybe you should. I know you said you're not interested in dating but maybe you should be."

Alice had noticed the missing ring and he was very attractive, and Lisa might say she wasn't looking for a relationship but it might be exactly what she needed. The nudge of regret she felt about fixing her friend up with Seth was surprising. Startling, even.

What was that about?

"I'm not on the market. I told you before I didn't mind admiring a goodlooking man but that was it. So, I will admire him and might be tempted to go in the bathroom and watch him tear that tile out. But only because I like to watch a strong man working, all those muscles rippling." She grinned impishly. "But no, no, no. I was not kidding when I said I'm not on the market. Remember I mentioned I had tested those waters in France, and it was a disaster. I don't have the energy yet to tackle the drama of a relationship."

"You did mention it but haven't told me about this mystery man with whom you had this disaster." Alice studied her friend. "Was he terrible? You can't let him, or Mason define the rest of your life. Yes, you've been through a drama-filled marriage ending, and then had some drama on a rebound relationship, it seems. Lisa, there are wonderful men out there. You just had a rough start."

Lisa frowned hard, a crease dividing her eyebrows. "Did you not hear the word no? And why are you talking about me? You're single."

Alice knew she'd pushed too hard and probably deserved Lisa's irritated response. "My situation is different. I'm not ready. I'm not sure if I'll ever be ready."

"Bingo. And I hate to remind you but it's getting close to two years since William died. Just a few short months to go. Maybe it's time for you to think about testing the waters. That man is going to be here for a couple of months, so maybe at some point, after we make double certain he really is a nice single guy, then you might be ready."

Alice bristled. "Maybe we need to talk about something else before he hears us." Alice just wanted the conversation to end. She glanced toward the hallway. It was a long hall and she could hear him loudly tearing something out, so he probably hadn't heard anything. Still, she didn't want to take chances because it would be far too embarrassing. "We're both starting fresh and I'll probably never be ready to remarry. Besides, I'm more interested in Jackson and Nina getting together. I think they're getting along really well. He took her horseback riding on our ranch today."

Lisa grinned. "Interesting. I'm thinking there's something brewing there."

Alice breathed a sigh of relief that she'd successfully changed the subject from her dating anyone. "I really hope so. I think they could be perfect for each other. I'm just a little worried. Nina doesn't talk much about her past. It's almost as if she is hiding something or not comfortable enough to open up. Do you get that feeling? I really don't want to encourage something between them, and Jackson get hurt in the end."

"Then maybe we need to up our game on pulling information from Nina. We can always ask her."

"I don't want to be intrusive. I enjoy her company. Maybe she'll open up with time."

"Maybe. We all move at our own pace. So, are you ready to bake?"

"More than ready."

"I thought we'd bake some cannoli."

"That sounds delicious. And Seth said he would be glad to be a test subject."

"A testing subject." Lisa smiled a bit wickedly. "That sounds far too tempting." She chuckled and turned to grab the dishes she would need.

Alice just stood there, thinking of Seth being a tempting test subject... *Test subject for what?*

Kissing?

Hugs?

All of the above?

Disturbed by her thoughts and guilty of thinking them, she grabbed up the cannoli recipe. Cannoli was the only testing she was doing today—or any day.

CHAPTER FOURTEEN

Jackson was still thinking about Nina saying she was interested in him as they rode around the rocks that hid the swimming hole from view. He didn't have to look back at her to know when she saw the lake. Her gasp told the tale, just as he'd expected it would when she saw the swimming hole. "So, what do you think?"

"I-it's like a mirage or something."

It was in many ways like a mirage. The land was flat to a certain point, and then the rocks began until there was the hill that was gradual, and then the larger rocks that came out of nowhere. When you went around them, there was a backdrop on one side of thick scrub brush and a deep chasm that cut through the land. At its base down below was a beautiful, cool, sparkling water hole that had rocks that led down to it and a small waterfall that made it always filled with fresh water and always perfect for swimming.

"Do you swim in that?" She looked at him with wide eyes.

"Yes, we do. I should have told you to bring a swimsuit. But when it was just us boys growing up, we didn't really worry about them."

She laughed. "Well, right now I would have to worry about it, but I can see where you guys probably didn't. That is just gorgeous and you're right, I can see the painting. Maybe when I come to paint it, I can swim."

"You could. Come on. Right now, you could put your feet in it, even if you don't want to swim?" He grinned at her. He didn't figure she'd take the bait, but he had to throw it out there.

"Not hardly. I'm assuming that Jackson McIntyre is no saint with that little mischievous suggestion, not in so many words."

He grinned again, enjoying teasing her. "I never said I was a saint. I try to be a gentleman, though, so you don't have to have any worries."

"It's true, you have been very gentlemanly, and it feels genuine. Now, how do we get down there?" She pointed to the water. "My toes are itching to be in that cool water."

"I'm very genuine, Nina. I hope you know that."

She stared at him then nodded. "Good to know."

Not exactly the enthusiasm he was hoping for. "Follow me." He led the way, taking his horse down a sloped path, and she followed him. He looked over his shoulder. "The mare is calm and you should feel safe."

"I'm feeling pretty good."

Jackson glanced over his shoulder again and several times more to encourage her. "You're doing great." And when he made it to the bottom, he turned his horse to wait for her. "There you go. You are a horsewoman after all. I think you were telling me a little lie there."

She laughed. "I swear, I haven't ridden in years and never on an incline like that. It's just this horse—she's amazing."

"I have to say Hilde is that, but you did great too. And you weren't scared?"

"I wasn't. But to be honest, I think that was because you gave me such a good horse and I could feel her confidence. And also, you were here."

Jackson dismounted and let his reins drop to the ground because the horses weren't going anywhere but to the water as quickly as they could get to it. He moved to Nina. "Let me help you down."

"Thank you." She pulled her leg over the horse, then placed her hands on his shoulders as he wrapped

147

his hands around her waist and eased her down so she stood next to him.

It was very hard to let go. She smelled of some sweet scent that drew him like a bee to pollen, and his gaze dropped to her lips. When he realized what he was doing, he met her gaze.

"You are very tempting, Nina Hanson," he said, his voice husky even to his own ears. He felt so drawn to her. He could see her thoughts whirling behind those beautiful eyes of hers.

She swallowed hard. "I think we better put our toes in the water."

She moved away from him. He told himself he might have moved faster than he should have. He hadn't been this attracted to anybody in a very long time, if ever, he realized. *What was it about Nina?* Something special and he didn't want to run her off. He also wasn't ready to hear the wrath of his mother if they got back from this trail ride and Nina never wanted to see him again.

That wouldn't quite be the ending that he wanted, and his mama would never let him live it down.

He followed Nina to the water's edge. She slipped out of her tennis shoes, set them to the side, then pulled her socks off and dropped them on top of the shoes. She chose a wide rock to sit on and rolled her pant legs up, not looking at him, and then she placed her feet in the water. He smiled, watching her expression as her feet hit the cold creek-fed water.

"This is heavenly."

He breathed a sigh of relief, seeing that she no longer looked tense. "Mind if I sit beside you?"

"No, not at all."

He sank down onto the rock and pulled his boots off, then his socks before rolling his jeans up.

Her chuckle had him glancing at her. Her eyes sparkled and her smile enticed him.

"I guess I don't often think about cowboys with their boots off."

He chuckled, thinking she was cute, and placed his feet into the clear water beside hers. "They're pretty awkward to sleep in. Or swim in."

"I can only imagine." She looked around and placed her fingertips under her thighs. "Y'all are so lucky to have this place all to yourselves. It's like your own little secret."

He breathed in the fresh air and looked around, taking in the feeling and atmosphere surrounding them. "We are, I'm not going to deny it. I've always been thankful for the life I was born into. This wild land is a part of me, and my brothers too."

"Do you bring others out here often? It's such a beautiful place, it's almost too good not to share. But then, it's also too special to share at the same time."

"Yeah. Very seldom do we bring anyone else here. I've never brought anyone here. My brothers have brought female friends out sometimes. It makes for a great date." He blanched. "I didn't mean to assume…"

"That this is a date. Is this a date?" She looked impish, enjoying his discomfort.

"Would you want it to be?" He put the ball back in her court. "I did ask you if you wanted to come riding and you did say yes, so I guess it could be classified as our first date." And there it was, out in the open.

No sense not testing the waters.

"To be honest, Jackson, I haven't had the best of luck with men. I was even surprised I agreed to come riding with you today. It's the first time I've done anything like that in three years."

"Really?" He had believed she'd been isolated, and he had been right. The idea bothered him.

"I felt comfortable doing that with you, though, and to be frank, it startled me. I've sworn off men. And all this time I've never been tempted to change that."

Her words settled in like a lump in his stomach. "I see. You must have loved your husband very much. And that's a good thing. I know with grief like my mom is going through… I'm learning that even with myself, it's not something that you can put a date on when it will end." *Or the guilt.*

She bit her lip, studied the water, and he could do

nothing but watch her, wishing he could read her thoughts.

She took a deep breath and turned to meet his gaze. She looked conflicted.

"See, that's where my story gets mixed up. I wasn't actually married that long. Just a little over two years. And my husband wasn't exactly who he had led me to believe he was... He was very controlling. And threatening. I went through a lot of emotional abuse for most of the marriage. I had finally had all that I could take. I left him—or tried to. It wasn't easy. He threatened me, that if I went through with the divorce, there would be consequences." Her gaze faltered, and she looked down at her lap.

Jackson's fury had risen the instant he realized she'd been abused. "Did he hurt you?"

"I had moved out and he was furious and found out where I was housesitting for a friend and taking care of her dog. Greg came and tried kicking in the door. The dog was barking but it wasn't stopping him. He kept kicking and I called 911 but then he broke a window. Thank God for the dog. She was a large German Shepherd mix and bit him before he could get in the window. By then we could hear the sirens and he told me he was going to get me and ran to his car. He left, and crashed into an embankment when his car skidded out of control trying to get away from the cops." She let out a shuddering breath. "And I became a widow."

Silence echoed between them. And his insides had twisted into a hard fist. He couldn't speak at first.

She spoke before he did. "Jackson, I haven't shared that with anyone. It's just too personal and painful." She looked suddenly full of trepidation. Her eyes narrowed. "I dated once after that and it didn't turn out so well either. So here I am at Star Gazer Island, in my own little world, minding my business and keeping a low profile. And I like it that way. I've had enough drama for one lifetime."

Maybe that was why he sensed more fire and vigor in her sometimes than normally. It was almost as if she subdued a personality that he got flickers of sometimes. Or maybe it was just that he was hopeful that he brought that out in her.

"That's horrible for you. First that you had to go through that. What about your family? Your parents, grandparents. Did you have anyone to help you?"

"My mother was a single parent and died in a car wreck on a tall bridge. I was in the car with her.

His face went white. "This is just too much. No wonder you have a fear of bridges. I am so sorry. How old were you?"

"Six. I have a hard time talking about it still. That, I haven't overcome. I spent an hour trapped inside the car, hysterical and knowing my mom was gone. My grandmother raised me and passed away my senior year of high school. She left me her house and a little inheritance, so I was able to finish school on my own. I always had painted and was content to be in my own little world with my paints. Painting was my therapy after the wreck and it's been a part of my life ever since. Being a loner has always been part of my life also. As you can see, my ventures past that have not been positive."

He still looked stunned and she felt stunned by everything and yet she was glad she'd opened up to him about all of her past. It felt right.

He touched her arm, rubbing it gently, comforting her. "I hope you know I would never share your personal life with anyone. But, it sounds like you could use some friends. I'm glad my mom moved in next door to you. She would never betray you. I wouldn't either. And Nina, if you ever need anything, all you have to do is ask and I'll help you."

She smiled at him. "Thank you. It's hard for me to open up. My life seems like a tragic made for television movie and I really, really wish it didn't."

"Well, maybe your future will be better."

* * *

They'd turned on the music as she and Lisa worked to prepare the cannoli shells and a variety of fillings. They had fun, talking about Lisa's travels and the chefs she'd baked with in Italy and France, where she'd spent most of her time taking cooking and baking classes with famous chefs. They tested different variations of those recipes.

"This is fun," Lisa said as she placed the trays in the oven. "I do love baking with friends." She then prepared them both a mimosa, an orange juice with a splash of champagne.

They sipped their drinks, enjoying their task of creating the fillings. The delicious scents and the beauty of the blue ocean outside the wall of glass leading to the veranda was perfect.

When they had the cannoli filled with the different fillings, they dipped them in different glazes and dustings of powdered sugar. It was testing time. She placed several on a plate and headed down the hall to give the hardworking Seth the promise of testing the pastries.

He smiled when she tapped on the door. He stood in the old pink bathtub with a wrench out as he worked on removing the showerhead. "You two ladies have been torturing me. The house smells amazing. Are those your creations?"

A warm zing of happiness filled her as she held

the plate out to him. "Yes. Cannoli. There are several different flavors. Nutella—much loved in Sicily, so it couldn't be missed—and Oreo for fun and love. And strawberry cream cheese with a twist. And last but oh so delicious, the sweet buttercream drizzled with lemon glaze."

His eyes widened and her smile warmed. She loved baking for her men—not that he was one of her men, she added to herself quickly. Her sons and her husband. She'd loved baking and cooking for them. She hadn't done as much since William had died but had let Rose, their housekeeper take over. But today it had felt good. "Please try them all and give us your opinion. I know you probably won't eat them all now, but I'll wrap up some for you to take home with you to enjoy later."

He stepped out of the bathtub and quickly washed his hands. Then he reached for the plate. Their hands brushed as he took it. He sank down to sit on the edge of the tub and studied the cannoli. He looked up at her. "Which is your favorite?"

She relaxed against the doorframe. "No, this is your opinion I'm interested in. We can do all of these as a dessert for the inn but we're looking for a signature dessert."

"Fair enough." He picked up the Nutella first.

The chocolate treat was delicious, she knew, but

155

her favorite was the buttercream and lemon.

His lips turned up happily as he chewed. When he was finished with that bite, he took one of each one. "Those are amazing. I've never had a cannoli before, but if you put that on the menu, I'll be eating here maybe several times a week. You did an incredible job."

A lovely feeling of delight flowed through her. "It was Lisa, mostly. She's the really talented one."

"You're humble too. I like that." His eyes held hers for a moment and then, as if realizing he might have crossed a line, he stood. "I, ah, I think the buttercream is my favorite. It is something light and not too heavy. I could eat several. The Nutella would be my second choice, but I would gladly devour each and all of them."

She took the plate when he held it out to her. "Thank you. I'll wrap you up some to take home. Would you like a cup of coffee, water? You could take a break and sit on the veranda for a breather. You've been busy in here."

"Coffee would be great. And I wouldn't mind finishing at least one of those—maybe two."

She smiled and led the way down the hall. Lisa looked up from drizzling caramel over another tray of the Nutella. "Seth, this is Lisa Blair, the talent behind the food."

156

He held out his hand and they shook. "Nice to meet you. These are delicious. I'm a fan."

Lisa took him in with a wide smile. "It's nice to meet you too. So, which is your favorite?"

"It might not be the manly choice but the buttercream nudges ahead of the others. That Nutella comes in a close second but like I told Alice, I'd eat them all and be grateful for it."

Alice chuckled as she reached to pour him a cup of coffee.

Lisa clapped her hands. "Wonderful. That is our favorite too. We'll do some more testing, but I believe we have a contender for the signature dessert. We'll be sure and give you a chance at the end of our testing to cast another vote."

"Great. I didn't know when I took this job I was going to get such a delicious bonus with it."

Alice held the cup of coffee out to him. "Cream and sugar are there on the end of the island if you want that. And we're glad you helped us out on the renovation and the cannoli. Please, go sit down for a minute."

Buttercup had been taking a nap and went to stand by the door.

"I believe someone else needs to go outside too." She reached for her leash, snapped it in place and opened the door. "I'll be back in a moment, Lisa."

"Take your time. I'm just finishing up this last batch."

She glanced over her shoulder at Lisa, and her friend winked and mouthed, "Enjoy yourself."

Denial rose instantly but as Seth followed her outside, she couldn't deny that she was enjoying his company.

* * *

Seth held the plate in one hand, the coffee mug in the other as he walked out onto the wide veranda that stretched all across the back of the inn. The place was amazing. He took a drink of his coffee and then set it down on one of the tables as he picked up one of the cannoli and took a bite. Alice came outside with the dog. She was a beautiful woman but, in the short time he had been working for her today he had been drawn to her. She'd seemed sad when she first opened the door to him but then when she and Lisa began baking in the kitchen, despite the door being closed most of the time, he'd heard their laughter.

He enjoyed hearing the sound of a woman's laughter again. It was one of the main things he missed about his wife. He wondered if Alice missed that about her husband. He had come here knowing she was a widow. And after spotting what looked like tears in her eyes he became committed to helping her reach her dream of remodeling this old inn and taking it back to its life.

He finished his cannoli and nodded toward the garden as she paused on the edge of the steps. "Are you taking the dog for a walk on the beach?"

"I am. Nina's not comfortable letting her run around without a leash yet. She's terrified that Buttercup will run off and then we won't be able to find her, so I have to walk her."

He rubbed the back of his neck, feeling a burn of nervousness. He wasn't used to this feeling...it had been a very long time since he'd felt anything remotely like attraction to a woman. "Would you mind if I walked with you?"

She looked a bit startled. "That would be nice. I'm sure you would like to have some time out of that house. And what better way to take a break than with a walk on the beach."

He got the feeling that she was as nervous as he was. He told himself that it had been five years. Five years since his wife, Jen, had passed away. And yet he had not dated. Hadn't been able to bring himself to do that. He met with friends sometimes and his friends often tried to fix him up but he just couldn't do it. So why was he looking at Alice and thinking...or feeling nerves? Why was he feeling attraction?

And what was he thinking, anyway? Her husband had only been dead less than two years. He had read about William McIntyre's shocking accident. A well-seasoned cattleman who knew better than to ride off into a deceptively calm river right after a raging flood. He'd been dragged under by something, a tree branch or barbed wire. He couldn't remember specifically, but he remembered wondering why a man like him who knew better had made such a mistake.

He set the plate on the table and picked up the last cannoli in one hand and his mug of coffee in the other and followed her down the steps. Walking beside her made him even more aware of her small stature. Jen had been tall, almost as tall as him. Looking down at Alice it was hard getting used to someone who looked like they were barely five foot one or two and here he was six-one. Kissing her could be awkward. And why was he thinking about that?

Gosh, his mind was playing crazy on him. "There's a lot of area out here. Are you thinking about adding anything? I remember there was a gazebo over there at one time."

She smiled up at him. "There was. And they had weddings there. But I think it must have rotted or something because it's not there anymore. I've thought about rebuilding it but instead of a gazebo it could be a small pavilion. I would love to hold small weddings here. And my brain is working overtime. I think if the inn does well that maybe expanding the wedding venue, maybe a pavilion at the ranch. We can handle the plans and have the larger weddings there. I'm sorry, why am I bothering you with all of this?" She started walking, letting Buttercup finally have her way as she sniffed the ground and plowed toward the beach.

He fell into step with Alice. "It's okay. It's good to think out loud. And I like what you're thinking. I can tell you're really enjoying yourself."

"I am. I needed this. I couldn't remain stagnant. I felt this immense tension building in me since losing William. And I just had to make a move. I needed something positive to pour myself into, to vent my mind."

They stared at each other and he understood all too well the need to be busy. He'd been the same way after Jen's death.

"I get that." More than she knew. He could tell her about Jen but Alice needed this time to talk so he let her. He was pleased that she felt comfortable enough with him to talk.

They reached the picket fence, and he opened the latch and Buttercup charged forward. Alice laughed and drew back on the leash to regain some control of the growing puppy. She looked at him after they'd walked a few feet into the bright sunlight.

"So will you build the platform?"

"I could draw you up a plan. Give you a quote. Then we can talk about it and you fill me in on what you want, and I'll make it happen after I finish the inside." He liked the way her face lit up when he said that.

"I think that sounds perfect. Seth Roark, I'm very glad that you got recommended to me for this job."

He had just popped the last of the cannoli into his mouth and finished it off. "And as you can see, I'm very glad I am here too." They reached the water and Buttercup frolicked in the shallow waves at the edge of the water.

Alice sighed. "Oh to be so carefree."

He heard the longing in her voice as she watched the puppy playing. "So I bring my boat out here a lot of times in the evening. Before you bought the inn I'd stop right out there." He pointed toward the sea. "I would stare up here and consider buying it myself. But then I'd talk myself out of it because with my business I stay busy and I didn't really want to take on a project this big. Besides, I think it's better with somebody who wanted to renovate it and open it back up. So I'm looking forward to everything you're going to do to it. And I was in town the other day and people kept asking about it. Everyone in this small town is excited about the remodel."

"That's wonderful." She tilted her head to the side. "You act like you're very familiar with Star Gazer Island."

He squinted in the sun at her. "Did I not tell you I live here?" He knew he hadn't told her.

"No, you did not tell me that. So you live here on the island?"

"Yes, I do. That's why I made my first meeting with you late in the day because I was finishing up a job in Padre Island. It gave me time to get back here from the job site and after I talked to you I went down the street and around the corner to my house."

"Isn't that something? Do you work on the island a lot?"

"Small jobs. This is the biggest job I've taken on in a long time. I have a very successful company, but I don't need it or want it to get huge. I do it to keep myself busy. And because I like working with my hands. Gives me joy."

"That's wonderful. So, I'm glad I can give you a job that keeps you home for a little while."

"And I thank you very much for that."

"And does that allow you time to get out on your boat more?"

"It does. I spend a lot of time there."

She stared out at the open water and breathed

deeply. "That sounds lovely."

"Any time you'd like to go, just let me know. I'd be happy to take you out. On the water," he added quickly, knowing instinctively she would turn down the take you out comment if not clarified.

Her expression turned wishful and then thoughtful. "Thanks, but as lovely as it sounds I have too much to do and speaking of, I better get back to work. As much as I love design, making certain each of these rooms has a color palette and bedding that sets it off is a job. Plus, Lisa might want to ask my thoughts on a recipe."

"I'm certain it will be perfect. And I need to get back as well. Your bathrooms are waiting." He'd thrown out a line, and she'd turned him down, just as he'd suspected. But he hated it, knowing that she would enjoy a relaxing ride on the bay and maybe watching a sunset. Maybe he'd clarify again at some point that it would be just between friends. Because he was certain that was what Alice needed right now.

CHAPTER FIFTEEN

Late Saturday morning, Nina headed over to see the progress being made on the inn and to have brunch with Alice and Lisa. She adored Alice and liked Lisa very much; she was bright and funny and incredibly talented, and had prepared several dishes for testing. Nina was on board with the testing, especially when she learned one of the dishes would be lobster quiche. She loved seafood and lobster was a favorite. She was going to enjoy this testing phase and loved that Alice and Lisa wanted to include her in their decision.

On Thursday, after their horseback ride, a ride she was still mulling over, Jackson had followed her back to visit his mom. Alice had brought Buttercup out to her, along with a plate of cannolis for her and one for Jackson. She'd instructed each of them to let her know which was their favorite. They had been delicious but she'd stretched eating them out over two days. She needed something to pamper her distressed nerves after her ride with Jackson. After she'd admitted to him that she was attracted to him.

Why had she done that? It was a mystery to her, especially considering she had been playing it safe and staying away from men for the last three years. So why, oh, why could she not keep from opening her mouth around him and spilling her guts, saying things better left unsaid? Feeling both tempted and depressed by her actions, she'd wallowed in the idea of eating every delicious morsel of the cannoli, and it had been a satisfying experience. But in the end, she still had no answer for why she opened up to Jackson the way she did. Something about Jackson McIntyre simply drew her to trust him. And as dangerous as she knew it was, she couldn't seem to help herself.

This morning's tasting test and chatting it up with her new friends was the distraction she needed from thoughts of Jackson. Jackson and the kiss she'd thought he was going to give her after she'd admitted to him that she liked everything about him. But he hadn't. After saying nothing for a long moment, as their gazes locked together, he'd smiled and told her he liked her very much and taken her hand in his. They'd enjoyed the rest of their time at that spring-fed swimming hole; then he'd followed her home and his mother had brought them the desserts. If he'd had any plan to kiss her when he followed her home, that had been nixed with the appearance of his mother. And thank goodness Alice had shown up, because the last thing Nina needed was to kiss Jackson.

She knew this, and yet, she kept thinking about it. Wondering. And wanting it.

Pushing the thoughts aside, she hurried through the side gate and down the flagstone path to the wide veranda. Alice had praised Lisa's skills in the kitchen and the cannoli had not disappointed. They'd been magical and besides anticipating more amazing food, Nina enjoyed the two friends. She could envision the two wealthy women having the time of their lives entertaining guests who came to the Star Gazer Inn. She knew it would be a grand success.

She tapped on the glass door of the veranda.

Alice waved her inside. "Come in. Where's Buttercup?"

"Home, curled up, taking a nap."

"She's a delight. I really enjoyed her being my shadow the other day. And she didn't get in the contractor's way at all. She went to the bathroom door and peered in a couple of times, but I think she didn't want any part of the ripping-out process."

"I'm so glad she behaved well and didn't get in anyone's way." She saw the spread of food on the bar. "Everything smells delicious."

Lisa beamed as she set a white dish of bubbly quiche on the end of the island beside a plate of assorted fruits. "Thank you. It is time to sit down and enjoy. Plus, there is coffee or pineapple-orange juice mimosas that are delicious." She waved toward the champagne glasses filled with the sparkling orange cocktail. She picked up a glass and held it in the air. "To having a good time choosing the inn's menu."

She and Alice picked up a mimosa and held it to join Lisa in the toast.

"To an exciting time," Nina said.

"To new beginnings," Alice added, and they clinked their glasses together and then took a sip and smiled.

After the toast, they filled their plates, then took seats outside at the table that Alice had set with a tablecloth, cloth napkins, silverware, and a vase of freshly picked pink periwinkles.

"Now, we want to hear all about your horseback ride with Jackson." Alice smiled apologetically. "I know he's my son, but we're curious about how you and Jackson are getting along. I can't help it."

Nerves raced through her at the thought of talking

to Alice about Jackson.

Lisa laughed. "First we eat. This quiche is fabulous, and the other dishes are all those I love. Plus, there's orange juice, coffee, more mimosas, if you'd like—whatever you want. We're getting this inn going and we're testing out all kinds of things. It is exciting."

"Oh," Nina gasped after her first bite of the lobster quiche. "This is to die for."

Lisa smiled in delight. "I am so glad you like it."

"I love it. Alice, you are right—you're blessed to have Lisa in the kitchen. So, it's just the cream cheese and peppers and eggs...and garlic. What's the secret?"

Lisa's eyes twinkled. "Hey, a woman has to have a few secrets. And believe me, I have them—both in the kitchen and out of the kitchen." She grimaced at the last statement and Nina could have added that she did too. "I've cooked all over the world. Everywhere I've traveled—Greece, Italy, France, to name a few— I've taken cooking courses with very famous chefs. So, I picked up a few little secrets."

"And she never gives those secrets away," Alice said. "Which always made all of her friends clamor to her parties because we knew what a treat it would be. When she called the day I was looking at starting to search for a chef, it just made sense. It's like fate brought us together."

Lisa laughed, and Nina did too. "I think that that's

going to be in your favor now. Because nobody but Star Gazer Inn will have Lisa. She'll be your secret weapon."

Alice chuckled and took a sip of her mimosa. "That's exactly what I'm hoping. The dining area of the inn isn't all that big but I'm thinking about enlarging it. There is a maid's quarters that backs up to the dining room and I've talked to Seth about knocking out the wall and he says it would be an easy project. And there is a lot of land here with the inn, so enlarging the veranda to include a patio for more tables would work well for summer, especially. I just have to see how well received we are and if the area can sustain a restaurant."

Nina looked out on the yard. "Wow, you really are looking for something to keep you busy. It sounds great but like a lot of work."

"Then there's the wedding gazebo and wedding planning she's been thinking about." Lisa nodded for emphasis when Nina gaped at her. "Alice isn't planning on sitting on her laurels, as they say. Or letting me. But it's going to be fun and we'll hire help when we need to."

She stared at the two fifty-something women. "You two amaze me. I'm totally impressed."

"I'm restless and ready to see what I can do," Lisa said. "After my skunk of an ex-husband decided to trade me in for a younger model, literally, I was angry. Very angry and traveling was a way to run away and escape. I had fun, despite being lonely and angry. Cooking was a great distraction. And then…" She paused, and her expression tensed. "Well, then, I decided I needed more."

Nina couldn't help but wonder what Lisa had almost said and decided not to ask. One of those secrets, maybe. Again, she understood completely.

"We'll start slow and then see where we go," Alice said. "I'd hate to risk running Lisa off with too much work. And I've decided that this needs to continue to be fun, not crazy stressful."

"But a challenge never hurt anyone," Lisa added, as if not content to let the idea of expansion die.

Alice smiled. "I'm challenged enough right now." Then she picked up one of the rolls and broke it in half as she looked directly at Nina. "Now, about my Jackson. How are you two getting along?"

Nina set her fork down and took a deep breath. She had to be cautious for several reasons, considering she wasn't sure how Jackson would feel about her talking about him, especially with his mother. And because she wasn't comfortable with what she was feeling for Jackson herself. "It was so much fun. The ranch is gorgeous, and it was my first time to be out like that. I'm one of those who sees the countryside through the window of a car as I speed down the freeway. So, I truly loved it. And that spring-fed pond is amazing. He's going to take me out so I can take photos of it at sunset. He says it's amazing and I'm eager to paint it."

"That will be fabulous. It is such a beautiful place." Alice sighed. "It was one of mine and William's favorite places. I have very fond memories there. And the sunsets are not to be missed."

The love Alice had for her husband was evident and Nina suddenly, with all of her heart, wished she could have found such a love. *Was her chance truly over?* Jackson's image filled her thoughts and she felt that constant pull to test those deep fears that kept her drawn into herself.

Lisa looked suddenly as sad as Nina felt. "I do envy what you and William had, Alice. And I can't wait to see this painting, Nina." Tears filled her eyes, and because Nina and Alice sat on either side of her, they both reached and touched her arm, trying to comfort her.

"What's wrong?" Alice asked gently. "Is it something to do with Mason?"

She sniffed and looked embarrassed at the unexpected display of emotion. "No, my ex is a fool and I'm better off without him. It's just, foolish me getting emotional over you losing the love of your life, it's got to be hard. And then there is me, stuck with such a jerk always looking for ways to drag me down. It just makes me mad and sad...and angry that you lost William. Sorry."

Alice gasped. "I had no idea he was bothering you. And to be honest, I went through some anger at first myself over my big-hearted William dying. Thankfully, God got hold of my heart and gave me peace about that, I mean, we all have a time to die...and none of us know what the future holds or the reasons why things happen. Still, I just still miss him and I wanted him here with me. As for your ex, why on earth would he be trying to drag you down? He got what he wanted with his other family. Can't he just leave you alone and let you get on with your life?"

From what Nina had seen of Lisa, this show of emotions was very out of character and she was surprised by it. Nina hadn't believed that the tears were solely for Alice and William. Now she knew her hunch that Lisa had more going on in her past than she showed with her upbeat expression that she always seemed to have was correct.

"I'm sorry you're going through that," she said, thinking about her own experience with Greg and then with Joe. She pushed thoughts of him out of her mind, not ever wanting to go there. Just wishing with all of her heart that she'd never met the man who took what her husband had done to her and then finished off any trust of men she had left.

"He just despises me for reasons that are beyond me. I think maybe because I tried to go on with my life and didn't try to win him back. And that I took back my maiden name and now go by Blair. He made a comment about how fast I'd disposed of his name. It's just weird. Anyway, I'm fine. I'm stronger than he knows and he will not break me. I'm just rattled this morning because he texted some hurtful things yesterday, sent some pictures of him and Tabitha that were not really appropriate. And I thought I could let it slide but it keeps creeping into my mind and ambushing me. I'm fighting it off, it's just taking more of my will power than I'm wishing it did."

"What kind of pictures?" Alice looked appalled and Nina wondered if she was also worried that her friend was putting on more of a brave face than she was really feeling.

Nina hated to imagine, given her view of how awful men could be from her own personal experience.

"Let's just say they were of him and her frolicking on the beach and meant to make me feel inadequate. There were some before that were worse."

"That is pathetic. Can you turn him in? Call the cops. I'm so out of my element on things like this."

Lisa laid a hand over Alice's, which was still

laying on her arm in a comforting gesture. "Sweet friend, I never should have mentioned it. I'm going to continue to ignore him for now. He's really not worth the breath to turn him in, and I'm really not sure what they would do. I just want to go on, living my new life and letting the past grow smaller and smaller in the rearview mirror of my life. William and your relationship is an inspiration to me that there is still goodness and true love in this old, tainted world."

"Yes, it is," Nina agreed. And feeling compelled to open up to these two women who had opened up to her, she said, "Finding love like Alice had with William isn't that easy. To be frank, I told Jackson the other day that I was a widow. But I told him the whole story and I didn't tell you everything." They were looking at her now and she gave a small smile. "Alice, I was going to file for a divorce the next day but my husband was killed in a car accident after he tried to hurt me. I made a terrible judgment call when I chose to marry him. He was an emotional abuser, and I had finally gotten the courage to leave him and for that I'm grateful. I can look back and know that I had taken that step forward. However, since then, I have not talked about it. And I need to be truthful with you two, who have been so open with me. I really value that and have needed friends since being here.

"Alice and I may both be widows, but that's where

the similarities end. You were so very blessed, and I envy you that. But Lisa, it sounds like your story and my story are more similar, sadly. I really don't care to talk about it right now, but I made another bad judgment with a different man afterward. It's like I couldn't learn my lesson. But believe me, I have now."

Both women stared at her and she was both horrified that she'd exposed the truth but felt good about getting it out too.

"Yes, it does sound like we've both had issues," Lisa said. "I'm so sorry for you. Men can be such jerks. But Nina, you are too young to be so jaded. You have your entire life ahead of you. Don't let two bad seeds mess you up. And, that sweet Jackson is a real man." She hitched a brow, raised her mimosa and smiled. And just like that, Lisa was back to being her encouraging, positive self.

And she was obviously as good at shoving her pain beneath that façade as Nina was.

CHAPTER SIXTEEN

Over the next three weeks, Seth remodeled the kitchen at the Inn and Nina was invited over regularly to test delicious menu offerings that Lisa created in the renovated kitchen. Lisa knew her way around a kitchen. From tempting desserts that made her not care whether she'd gain ten pounds eating them, to the most delicious dinner entrees she'd tasted in her life the woman was a marvel in the kitchen. Creamy pasta with so many variations of mouth-watering sauces Nina's mind spun thinking about the entrees. And her stomach growled thinking about the appetizers she could have eaten all day: Homemade bruschetta with fresh picked tomatoes. Toasted almond-crusted brie topped with apricot-mango chutney on toasted rounds of buttery crackers…amazing!

On another day, it was blue corn-crusted redfish, a delicious redfish fillet over white cheddar grits and a basil-chardonnay sauce. Another day, it was a to-die-for spicy shrimp bisque and tarragon-sherry crème frappé toast that Nina had loved. Then there was the traditional but exceptional marinated beef flank steak, sautéed with savory green peppers and onions grilled to perfection and topped with a sour cream and avocado sauce that left you craving more.

One thing she knew was the dinner menu for the Star Gazer Inn was going to be eclectic and unforgettable. The lunch menu was going to draw women like moths to a flame, for the relaxed luncheons with its delicious sangrias, fresh salads, shrimp cocktails, and spoon drop crab cakes, with grilled shrimp topped with bisque sauce and a creamy lime sour cream. Her mouth watered remembering the amazing dish. Oh, yes, once the word was out, women would flock to the Star Gazer Inn for special get-togethers with girlfriends, showers, birthdays and just gossip-filled cocktail hours with their best buddies. It was happening and Nina had no doubt about it.

But the fun part was watching Alice and Lisa come alive in the kitchen, coming up with just the right combinations. They were so busy it seemed they had no time to be sad or let their past intrude, and Nina was glad. She wanted them to be happy, and though she didn't know for sure whether there had been other times like the day when Lisa had broken down and confessed what a jerk her ex was with his taunting, inappropriate photos, she thought her new friends were moving forward and she was so happy for them.

Then there was Seth Roark. The older man was seriously good-looking. She could only imagine that he probably would have been a cover model with his hard body and amazing physique when he was younger, not that the man acted like that would have ever been on his radar of bucket list items. But he was in his late fifties and hot. There was just no getting around it. Yes, she had to say that Jackson was one of the hottest men she'd ever been around; it was becoming increasingly difficult to hide her feelings for the man but Seth, as an older man, was a silver fox some would say, except the man's dark-brown hair only had a slight dusting of silver running through it. She wondered whether her friends had noticed that they had such a gorgeous hunk working wonders at the inn. Both Alice and Lisa would be contenders for the gentleman contractor's attentions, but she thought maybe Alice was better suited for the low-keyed heartthrob.

She knew that he and Alice were working closely

together on the renovation. But Alice seemed to be still grieving and uninterested. However, Nina found she was hoping that before Seth finished the renovations in the next few weeks that maybe something would happen between them.

Maybe it was just her romantic heart wishing that love could heal at least one of her friends' wounded hearts. And then there was her own wounded heart. She'd spent a little more time with Jackson and though there were times she'd thought he might kiss her, he didn't. She wasn't sure how she felt about that. She'd thought she wasn't interested in another relationship and yet every time she was near him, she knew she wanted him to make a move to take their friendship to another level.

This morning, with the sun streaming through the blinds of her bedroom window, Nina rolled over, content to sleep a little later this Monday morning. She had been up late finishing a painting, a painting she was very tempted to sign her name to. She had to stop being afraid at some point. Joe surely had moved on to other interests.

Buttercup jumped up onto the bed and placed her paws on Nina's chest. The golden pup barked happily. "I agree, Buttercup. It's going to be a great day in the neighborhood." She sat up and gave her puppy a scratch on the head. She was so happy to have her companion. She had been getting so lonely here before Buttercup came into her life, and Alice and Lisa.

And Jackson.

Jackson was taking her out to the peninsula where their cattle were ferried over to graze on the nutrient-rich grasses that grew there.

And on that note, she jumped from the bed and raced to the kitchen. Time for coffee, a cream cheese bagel and then a shower. Twenty minutes later, with a thick white mug filled with creamy coffee, she reached into her shower and turned on the water flow. She sipped her coffee while she waited for it to warm up. Then, setting her cup on the vanity, she stripped out of her pajamas and climbed beneath the spray. This was going to be a good day. She was going to test out not being wary of Jackson.

She had just poured herself another cup of coffee and was about to take Buttercup on a short walk along the beach so she wouldn't be restless on the trip when Jackson walked around the corner of her house. Delight raced through her at the sight of him. He was early.

"Hi," he said immediately. "I knocked but you must not have heard me. I thought I'd check and see if you were out here on the porch. Hope you don't mind."

"No, not at all. I was about to take Buttercup on a

short walk. You know, so she won't be too wound up in the truck. Want to come?"

"Sure." He walked up the steps and she was very aware of him as he bent to pet Buttercup, who was dancing with joy. "Hey, little lady, you are a happy gal today."

Nina's heart sighed watching him and her puppy. This man would be a joy to wake up with every morning. The thought startled her and jolted her. "Coffee. Do you want a cup?"

He looked up and gave her a sexy, lazy smile. "Sounds great."

She realized he looked a little tired. "I'll get it. Hold this." She held the leash that was already attached to Buttercup's collar out to him. Their fingers brushed and she let go immediately and hurried inside.

Feeling unsteady she pulled a thick mug from the cupboard and poured him a cup. It would just be a short walk so there was no need for either of them to have an insulated coffee mug. He was standing at the edge of the porch looking toward the water when she walked back outside, and her insides got weak and fluttery at the sight of him. He turned half toward her as she closed the door behind her, and her heart skipped a beat. She handed him the coffee and he took it, his eyes holding hers for a long moment.

"Thanks," he said finally.

It was as if she'd been holding her breath in those seconds. "You're welcome. Want me to take the leash?"

"Nope, I've got the wild one. You grab your cup of coffee and just enjoy the walk."

There was no doubt about that. She picked up her mug and they walked down the steps across the yard and through the gate to the sand. It was a perfect morning.

Later, after they'd drank their coffee and Buttercup had chased several seagulls, they took their empty mugs back to the house and then headed across to the inn. They'd not really talked about much, just looked for shells and laughed at the pup's antics. It had been a pleasant, easy exchange and one she enjoyed very much.

Seth Roark's truck was parked in the circle drive after they walked over so Jackson could say hello to his mother and Seth, whom he had met on an earlier trip into town. The inn was coming along. Seth had almost finished the downstairs bathrooms, and they were stunning. And Alice had painted several of the rooms downstairs, and every day, furniture deliveries or accessories were arriving. Alice bought some things at local stores, but she'd had to resort to searching online catalogs in the evening before she went to bed. She'd confessed to Nina that there weren't enough hours in the day and that she enjoyed being there when Seth was so she could see his progress. Lisa had laughed and teased her that she just loved watching Seth work or eat the food they asked him to test out for them. Nina had to admit that she hoped one day Alice might open her heart to love again and that maybe she and Seth could discover whether there was more to their relationship than remodeled bathrooms.

Wishful thinking on her part.

After taking the basket of goodies from a smug-looking Lisa, they drove an hour to the barge where the cattle were being loaded for the trip across the intercoastal.

"You look tired," she said, as he drove and she'd glimpsed the weariness again that she'd thought she'd seen earlier.

"It's just a busy time of year and I've just got my hands full."

"We could have put this off." She didn't want him to go out of his way to accommodate her if he didn't have time.

His gaze settled on her and she felt that undeniable desire to move closer to him.

"I wanted to see you."

Five simple words and her day got a lot brighter. "Really? I'm glad. I wanted to see you too." She laughed, knowing it was true. "Well, I was wondering if you had noticed that when I was out there the other day." She tried to tamp down the emotions inside her that were wishing that maybe she could be building a life with him. *Why was she having those thoughts?* She knew she wasn't ready for that. Had told him that. She was getting in deeper than she had wanted to, but this morning when they had walked along that beach together, she had felt so comfortable in his presence. And earlier, when she had handed him that coffee mug, standing there in that sunlight on her porch, she had momentarily had a flash of what it would be like waking up in the mornings with him, sharing coffee and breakfast or before they headed out for the day or went for a beach walk every day together. It was disturbing to her because it was so strong, and she couldn't get it out of her brain.

He slowed and as he turned onto a small two-lane road, he glanced at her. "I was going to ask you if you'd like to come to the cattle sale. It's a great night and in honor of my dad this year. Mom and Lisa will be coming too, and I know they'd love for me to invite you. Mom is probably just waiting to see if I invite you and if I don't, she'll do it anyway."

She stared at him, uncertainty gnawing a hole in her gut. Was it a date? How did she feel about that? But it was in honor of his dad. How could she turn that down? And was she using it as an excuse to say yes?

"I'd love to go." And there it was, she was going.

They reached the waiting barge, with its cattle pens made of what she assumed was iron railing. The cattle haulers were there, backed up and unloading the cattle, and she watched them cross the ramp onto the barge. "This is interesting." She was fascinated.

"It is, isn't it? There are many ways of doing it, but we've always used this barge service. Our grazing land is close to the ferry drop-off and our men—me, too, if I weren't being your tour guide today—will do an old-fashioned cattle drive from the drop-off to the grazing land. It's a short distance, but we all enjoy it."

"Kind of the Old West coming to life."

He chuckled. "Kind of. You'll get to watch when we unload. We'll follow in the truck."

"I believe that would make an amazing portrait. I'll be ready to snap some shots."

When the cattle were all loaded and the gates firmly locked, they motioned for Jackson to drive onto the barge.

"Let's get out. There is a walkway along the edge of the cattle pen."

They got out and, to her surprise, he took her hand and led her along the edge of the barge until they reached the front, where there was a bench.

Soon the barge was moving, and they stood at the railing, riding into the wind. The salty air invigorated her, and the sea spray gave a bit of a grittiness to her skin. She could see the shoreline and watched as it drew closer and closer.

"I see it." She looked out into the distance and she could see the dunes and the salt grass waving in the wind. It was very wild and rugged-looking with the rolling tall grass and cattle scattered over the land. "That is cool."

"I think so too. I thought you would enjoy seeing it." He smiled, and she responded with one of her own.

Feeling alive, though unsettled by the depths of Jackson's eyes, she looked back across the glistening water to the island. Her heart thundered and her fingers tightened around the railing, very aware that his shoulder and her shoulder brushed together with the shifting of the barge as it moved through the water.

The barge jerked as it slowed before docking. She was startled and lost her balance a bit, sidestepping to try to stay upright.

Jackson's hand instantly covered hers and held on and steadied her. "Steady there."

"Y'all okay up there?"

At the sound of a voice very much like Jackson's, she tore her gaze from Jackson to look across the cattle to a handsome rider. Tucker lifted a hand in greeting. She'd met Tucker when he'd dropped by the inn to check on Alice. She waved back.

"I didn't realize one of your brothers was along."

"One of us is usually always on the barge ride. We really enjoy the actual working the cattle part. The part we don't enjoy as much is the sitting behind the desk and these days, that tends to be more my problem than theirs. But then, I'm a homebody and don't like traveling all that much, so I like that part of being chained to the desk. So any excuse I can have for a day away from the computer is a good day. Like now, spending the day with you."

Wow. He did say the nicest things. "I'm glad I could help. I'm available anytime." Boy, she'd opened that door wide.

"And that sounds like a great invitation. I'm going to warn you now that I'll bc taking you up on your offer. We better head back to the truck so we can get ready to unload."

They walked back toward the truck and her mind reeled from what he'd just said. *He was going to call her.* And right now, as they walked to the truck, he was still holding her hand as if it were the most natural thing. She looked down at their clasped hands. She wanted to run her thumb over his. She looked up at him and found he was watching her. He smiled. And he didn't let go of her hand.

CHAPTER SEVENTEEN

Alice had decided to name each room after something to do with the beach: the Starfish, Seagull, Sandpiper, Sand Dollar, Beachcomber, Seahorse, Sunrise, Sunset. Ocean Breeze and Lighthouse rooms. She'd had fun ordering furnishings and accessories for each room. They were all done with a color theme in soft tones of sunset and sunrise colors. She'd bought paintings from Nina, having to force her to let her pay her for them, though Nina had tried to talk her into just letting them be in the inn on consignment. Alice had told her, "No, Nina, I'm selfish and love them and want to buy them. I'll gladly give them your card or better yet, give them a link to your website, if you would please set up a website."

Nina had looked away, almost at a loss for words before she'd finally said anything. "I'm just not comfortable with a website at this time."

And so, she'd let Alice buy the beautiful paintings and had asked Lisa if she thought there was something strange about the way Nina didn't sign her paintings and refused to even try to place any in the galleries in town. Lisa had agreed. Star Gazer Island was like so many small coastal towns, with quaint shops and art galleries. Both of them were certain that all of the galleries would be thrilled to offer Nina's beautiful paintings for sale.

Alice's thoughts were proven when earlier in the week, a local morning show had come to interview her about the reopening of the inn and she'd given them a tour. The television host instantly noticed Nina's art and instructed the cameraman to get them in the shots. The show aired yesterday and already Alice had been contacted by several online destination bloggers for more interviews and a interest in touring of the inn and each of them had commented on the gorgeous artwork. Several were coming out to interview her over the next week, to take photos to share with their readers.

Seth was trying hard to finish the upstairs bathrooms by then.

In the Sandpiper room, decorated in peach and sand tones, the gorgeous painting above the queen-sized bed was of a sunset shimmering over golden water and wet glistening sand, with two adorable, long-legged sandpipers chasing a tiny crab in the receding waters. It was a peaceful painting and Alice loved it.

"Alice, there you are." The deep voice of Seth had her swinging around.

Her handsome contractor was lounging with one shoulder against the doorframe. His muscular arms were crossed, bringing attention to his defined biceps and forearms. He watched her with those gentle blue eyes of his that seemed a deeper shade of sapphire today and she instantly got that light buzz of awareness that had been happening more and more when she was around him. She inhaled sharply but gave him a smile. "Here I am. Do you need me for something?"

His gaze locked with hers and for a moment they just stared at each other. It was a bit unnerving for her. She was very out of her element in moments like this. Thankfully, he shifted his gaze from hers and looked around the room.

"You've done a beautiful job in all of these rooms. I think this one is one of my favorites."

"Thank you. This one is my favorite. I love Nina's inspirational painting. There is just something about a cute sandpiper. They're just playful and busy, and I love watching them run down the beach on their little spindly legs." She laughed, thinking about the one she'd watched just that morning on her walk.

"I like that too. Kind of reminds us to take time to enjoy simple things. Like chasing crabs." He grinned and that buzz in the pit of her stomach moved to her chest.

She chuckled softly. "Maybe so. So, did you need me?"

A slow smile spread over his handsome face. "Come on, I need your opinion in the Sand Dollar room's bathroom." He turned and walked down the hall.

Alice followed him, admiring the way he moved. The man had a strong way of moving, intent and with purpose. He entered the room at the end of the hall and when she went in after him, he was waiting next to the bathroom. "Take a peek and let me know what you think about the floor-to-ceiling cabinet. And I've finished the tile."

Her eyes widened as she entered the bathroom. He'd worked a miracle, making the room seem larger than it was. He'd torn out the old, outdated bathtub and the small square tiles in a dusty blue and miles and miles of grout. And he'd replaced it with a walk-in shower with large cream plank tiles, really fancy multi-jetted showerheads to make the shower spa worthy, and enclosed it with a glistening glass wall that allowed the room to be open and seem bigger. Dark wooden cabinets had been replaced with very sleek, creamy white cabinets and added to the clean, open lines. The sparkling nickel fixtures and hardware finished off the look. The floor tile was a patterned hand-painted tile of blue and cream, and the walls were painted a soft vanilla ice cream-toned paint named Greek Villa.

"It's perfect," she uttered, totally in love with the look of it. She clasped her hands together, holding them below her chin as she took it all in. Then she looked at Seth. "You are making my dream come to life. This is just beautiful. Like the bathrooms downstairs, these will thrill my guests."

He smiled. "Thank you, but you picked everything out. It's your design. I just executed your design and it is good. Very good."

She liked his humble attitude. She knew good and well that he'd helped guide her in the choices for the high-end shower fixtures that would satisfy her guests. "We did good."

His smile warmed her through and through, and they stared at each other.

"Well, I need to go a little early today."

There was a heaviness to his voice. "Sure. Is something wrong?" She searched his face deeper now.

He gave a flatlined smile that was not happy or

sad, but somewhere lost in between. "It's the death date of my wife. I always take flowers to her grave."

Her heart clenched and she closed her eyes for a moment before looking at him again. "I'm so sorry. I do the same thing on William's death date. On his birthdate, too. What was her name, your wife?"

There was a look of relief on his face now. "Jennifer. I called her Jen."

"How long ago did you lose her?"

"Five years. How long has it been for you?"

"One. Well, seventeen months, to be exact. And William's death date was just as hard as his death had been. Is it still that hard for you after five years?"

"Not as hard, but it's hard. When you love someone, you never forget, and your body knows when special days are approaching. Especially the death date."

"Yes, I found that out. In March, when his birthday was coming, I had days that I felt in a fog and my heart was so heavy. I came here to the beach nearly every day and walked the beach."

"Walking is good. I work. Keep busy and try not to think about how much I miss her. Jen would have loved your inn."

This touched her. "I'm glad. Part of that would be because she loved your work, I'm sure."

He smiled and it warmed her heart again. "She's

actually the one who told me I should follow my dream, my bliss." He chuckled. "Those were her words. I'd have never used the word bliss, but she was right. Working with my hands has been part of what has helped me get through losing her."

"You weren't a contractor before Jen's death?"

"No, I was the CEO of a Fortune 500 company. She had cancer, and I left the company to be with her in the last six months of her life. She urged me not to go back. To instead do what I'd always wanted to do, build things. In the end, I started a small contracting company, working with my hands, working through the grief much like you worked through yours walking on the beach, I think."

They both inhaled, thinking in companionable silence. He understood what she was feeling, and Alice found comfort in knowing that.

"Well, I better go." He stepped back, out into the bedroom, and the bathroom seemed even bigger without his tall form beside her.

"Yes, of course." She followed him out into the Sand Dollar room and then continued past him into the hallway. He followed behind her as she walked down the hallway and then down the stairs. The old rug was worn in places. He was going to remove the carpet and redo the treads before he finished his remodel, but they had decided that would be the last thing he did before finishing his renovation.

Maybe it was because she was lost in thought, thinking about Seth losing his wife and knowing grief as deeply as she did, but halfway down, her toe caught on one of the threadbare spots and she stumbled. She cried out, panic filling her. She grabbed for the stair railing and missed. Suddenly, Seth's strong hand wrapped around her waist and he pulled her hard against his body.

"I've got you." His voice was gruff and strong, and wrapped around her in reassuring waves as she looked up into his face.

Her heart thundered, raced like a thousand jackhammers and she flushed, feeling her skin heat. So many thoughts flashed through her mind as he held her. "Thank you," she said, breathless as emotion swirled inside of her. "I wasn't paying attention." Embarrassed and feeling weak in the knees as his eyes bore into hers, she reached to grasp the banister. To pull away, to stand on her own.

He let her go but held onto her shoulders until he knew she had the banister for balance. "I'll pull this old rug up in the morning. That's more dangerous than I thought. We can't have you getting hurt."

Her cheeks heated at her clumsiness. "Thank you. That was scary. I just wasn't paying attention."

They finished the trip down the stairs, and she

breathed easier once her feet were on the ground.

"I hope your visit goes well," she said, feeling awkward. She wasn't sure why—yes she was, it was her reaction to him when he'd simply grabbed her to save her from what could have been a disastrous fall. Anyone would have done the same thing if they'd been close enough.

"Yes, thanks. I'll head out now."

"Yes, of course." She watched him go and let out a sigh, feeling suddenly overwhelmed as the door closed behind him. Lisa was gone for the afternoon and she was glad. The silence of the old inn closed around her like a cocoon. She went to the kitchen and poured herself a glass of sweet iced tea, grabbed her sun hat from the hook and headed down the back steps, across the yard to the sand. She headed toward the water, and when she'd reached it, she sank into the sand, drew her knees up and settled in to watch the waves roll in.

Why was she so off-centered?

She knew exactly why: in the time since losing William, the only hugs she'd gotten from a man had been from her sons and they were not the same as hugs from William. She closed her eyes and felt Seth's arms around her, felt the pounding of her heart and that of his, because she realized that his heart had been pounding as furiously as her own. She told herself it was simply that Seth and William were similar in size and being in his arms had just been such a strong reminder of how it had felt to be in William's arms again. A place she had longed to be ever since he'd died. And yet she knew there was more to it. More than she was comfortable exploring.

She rubbed her temple, trying hard not to think about Seth anymore. But it was useless. She'd enjoyed the conversations she had with Seth, though there really weren't that many that hadn't had to do with the renovations. She did find him attractive. But what woman wouldn't? She wasn't interested in him though.

She had no plans to remarry.

No plans to date.

No plans of a romantic nature at all, going forward with her life.

She'd had the love of her life. She'd been blessed to have William in her life. But of everything they'd shared, she missed conversations with him desperately. Missed the feel of his arms around her. Missed being tucked into his side with one arm over her shoulders as they sat on the porch together in the evenings simply discussing their day. Tears welled in her eyes…she'd so taken those simple moments for granted.

She blinked back the tears and stared out at the waves as she heaved in a steadying breath. She sat far enough back from the water that she wasn't in the walkers' or joggers' way as they passed. For a moment, she let her gaze linger on a couple walking hand in hand. Her heart ached for what she'd had and lost.

Her thoughts went to Seth carrying flowers to Jen's grave. *Five years.* Seth knew the heartache. He understood and, for just that brief moment in time when he'd told her about Jen, it had felt good to know someone understood her heartache. It was a heartache only those who'd been through it truly could understand.

She felt sad for Seth and that death was what they had in common. And yet, it was an undeniable connection.

That had to be it. It couldn't be that she'd simply enjoyed the feel of being in his arms.

CHAPTER EIGHTEEN

They spent the afternoon on Whisper Island walking along the deserted beach, allowing Buttercup to run free along the coastline, her tongue hanging out from chasing seagulls and a happy glint in her eyes. Then, when Buttercup was tuckered out and napping under the shade of a tall bunch of salt grass, they'd spread a blanket on the sand and sat down to enjoy the picnic Lisa and Alice had prepared for them. There had been a nice bottle of Pinot Grigio, a very fancy tray of various crackers and cheeses, and an assortment of sandwiches cut into quarters and arranged on a tray with grapes and strawberries. They'd thought of everything and made it look very fancy. He'd laughed when they'd started pulling it all out and there was a note that asked them to enjoy themselves and give a review of their picnic basket as it would be an offering to the guests of Star Gazer Inn.

"This is perfect," Nina said, picking up a strawberry and taking a bite.

Jackson watched her, his gaze stuck on her mouth, the mouth he had been thinking more and more about kissing. "Perfect," he said as he held her gaze.

"So, that big vacant looking house there in the middle of this surprisingly flat land belongs to your family?"

He looked across the pasture at the structure. "It does. We let people come out to fish sometimes. Sometimes we come to fish. But as you can see it's nothing fancy. I'll take you over to look if you want. The house is made of planks and sits on those stilts as you can imagine because of bad weather. It's been rebuilt a few times after hurricanes but never been completely destroyed."

"That's amazing. What happens to the cattle in times like that?"

"We get them out as fast as possible. If we think the storm is coming, we send the barge and cowboys over to round them up. We don't wait too long."

Later, he'd taken her home and it had taken all of his self-control not to pull her into his arms and kiss her lips. Instead, he'd held her hand then given her a hug, tugging her close and kissing her forehead. "Come to the swimming hole with me tomorrow. Drive out and we'll swim. But bring your supplies and we'll stay through the sunset so you can paint it."

Her eyes brightened. "I would love that. I'll come out tomorrow just after lunch. Will that work?"

"I'll be waiting." He backed away, refraining from kissing her, afraid to mess up a great day.

Tomorrow couldn't get here soon enough.

* * *

He had been more than ready for Nina to arrive this morning and when she'd driven up the road, he'd let out a sigh. He'd had a bad night, having been up most of the night after the nightmare had returned. He'd been in a hole since losing his father. He spent many of his nights in his head going over and over the moments before his father rode his horse into the recently surging river. *Why hadn't he shouted louder? Why hadn't he reacted quicker and gotten to his dad faster?* He'd relived those moments so many times, but even in his dreams—nightmares, really—he never made it in time. No, it was always the same: his dad's eyes locked with his just before the river swallowed him up and he never resurfaced. His horse made it out, but not his dad.

Seeing Nina getting out of her car had driven away the nightmare. He knew he had done everything he could to get to his dad; it just hadn't been enough. And looking into Nina's eyes, he was able to be distracted by thoughts of her that at least gave him a reprieve from the nightmares.

Her smile had filled his heart and he knew...he knew that he needed to know everything there was to know about this lovely, intriguing woman.

Now, sitting by the pond, a fishing pole in his hand but with Nina on his mind, he studied her making brushstrokes on her canvas. She bit her lip as she painted. He enjoyed watching her and though he didn't want to ruin the moment, his curiosity got the better of him.

Instead of talking himself out of it, he set the fishing pole in the pole holder he'd staked in the ground in front of him and then he plunged forward with the question that had taken over when the nightmares of his father drowning had made certain that he wasn't going to get any sleep last night. "So, tell me why you don't sign your name on your paintings."

"I..." she began, then paused, looking away from him and across the pond before her shoulders relaxed and her gaze met his. "I guess you've figured out there is a reason?"

"Yeah. You're too good. Your work is excellent. I'm no art critic but I know quality when I see it. I had trouble sleeping last night and finally gave up and decided to look you up on the internet. I'm sorry if that's invading your privacy. I was just curious and needed a distraction. I hope that doesn't bother you. I probably shouldn't have. But I quickly found you. It's not like I had to dig very far to see that in the art world you go by N.R. Henson. I'd recognize your style anywhere. There were too many commonalties and then I saw a photo of you."

It hadn't been too hard to find N.R. Henson, well-known artist of Texas landscapes and seascapes. What had him worrying about her was that his thought that she was hiding from something was all the stronger now. Three years ago, N.R. Henson had disappeared from anywhere on the internet. There hadn't, as far as he could tell, been any of her artwork sold and it couldn't be found in any galleries. *What happened to her three years ago?* Her husband had been dead for a little over four years, so what had happened a year after his death? Why had she gone into hiding on Star Gazer Island?

Holding his gaze, she moistened her lips and looked as if she were guilty. But what of?

She sighed and put her paintbrush into the jar of soaking solution and faced him. "It's embarrassing and scary at the same time. I should have already told you this, but I haven't talked to anyone about my past in so long that I had to be sure."

"Sure? About what?"

"Three years ago, after I'd been a widow for a year, I got involved with a man. Turns out he was a scam artist. He won my trust then stole from me. And then started threatening me."

Anger swept through Jackson in a wave. *Scammed? To what extent? And why was she hiding like he still suspected she was doing?*

* * *

Nina had felt self-conscious painting in front of Jackson but that didn't even begin to compare how embarrassed she felt now with him looking at her in shock. She'd been stupid when dealing with Joe, and it was terribly hard to admit to anyone what a fool she'd been. It was especially hard to admit it to Jackson. And the moment she'd started talking about it, he'd started frowning. She wanted to stop, to keep the rest to herself, but she forced herself to continue. If he thought less of her, then that was what she would have to deal with. She just needed to get this off her chest.

"I don't sell paintings anymore and I don't put my name on them because I'm afraid somehow, word would get out. You saw that I have built up a small name for myself. It's made me a comfortable living but I'm afraid he is watching for my work to resurface."

Jackson stood and his chocolate eyes were black beneath the shadow of his Stetson and the dip of his dark scowl.

Her heart pounded and her stomach cramped with worry.

"You think he's stalking you?"

She nodded. "I think he's looking for me to reappear somewhere. And I'm not ready to deal with him again." She moved to the large flat rock she'd been painting overhanging the water. She sank down on it and wished she could rewind time and never have met Joe. She couldn't bear to look at the disappointment in Jackson's eyes.

Jackson sat down beside her. "You're scared of this man? Afraid and hiding?"

She took a deep breath and looked at him. "Yes."

His expression was harsh but now it eased, and he gently pushed hair behind her ear and let his finger lift her jaw, so she looked more fully into his eyes. "You don't have to be afraid. Tell me what happened. I'm not happy right now but it's not you I'm angry at. It's this jerk. And I can promise you I'll get to the bottom of this. Now, tell me what happened."

Relief eased her embarrassment and the worry

cramping her insides. "I had a studio on the outskirts of Dallas—Plano. I started dating this man. I met him at my church, actually. He was really nice, or so I thought. He was new in town, but people liked him. When he helped me with a flat tire one day, he asked me out for a cup of coffee at the coffee shop. I went, and then I went out to dinner with him. At first, it seemed okay. We got along well and had a lot of the same interests. And then he told me he was having some financial problems and he needed a small loan. I gave it to him. As a loan." She inhaled a shaky breath.

"By that time, I had cooked dinner for him a few times. And then I'm not sure what happened, but he started coming to the house more often. He just slipped past my defenses. I guess I was more vulnerable than I realized. More foolish than I knew and…" She blinked back tears at having been such a fool. Oh, how stupid she felt. "I had an art show one night and he called and wanted to fix dinner for me. He'd done it a couple of times before and had my security code. I know, it was so stupid on my part, but I thought I knew him. It had been about six months and I thought…I thought I'd finally found someone I could love and who would treat me right."

"I'm sorry." Jackson's words were deep with emotion.

"Yeah, me too. I was wrong. When I got home,

there was no dinner and no him. And I soon learned that there was no money in my bank account. He somehow had gone through my things and using knowledge he had learned from me, he'd guessed my passwords and wired my money to an account that was cleaned out and closed before I even figured out that I'd been robbed."

"Wow. How much?"

"Thankfully, it wasn't everything, but it was a good eighty grand. It was money that I had saved, and it was going into my retirement fund. I had just been busy and hadn't put it in there. I reported him but he'd disappeared. The police told me he had done this before and that he'd targeted me."

"You were definitely targeted. Did they catch him?"

She shook her head, refusing to cry. "They never found a trace of him, but he started sending me threats. And it was clear that he was watching me, though I never saw him, and the cops didn't either. They could only do so much. Then he left me a note and told me that if I kept talking to the police, I'd be sorry. And to prove he wasn't kidding, he broke in and tore my home up and wrote on the mirror in lipstick that he was going to hurt me. I already wasn't sleeping or working, and he had scared me. I made a plan that day to leave and within a week, I'd hit the road. After a month of sneaking around and watching over my shoulder, I landed at Star Gazer Island."

He yanked his hat off and rammed a hand through his hair. "Wow. I've never dealt with anything like this before." He let out a long breath, as if thinking. "You've not heard from him in the last three years?"

"No. I searched the internet before I made my plan and learned how to disappear. It sounds foolish—he may not even be out there, but he scared me enough that I've disappeared."

"How do you live? Pay for things?"

"I live very carefully on cash. I use a throwaway phone and normally don't make calls. I don't make friends and keep to myself. I call the police chief on my case every few weeks to check in but so far, no luck. I've felt very alone. I've just quietly been living in the shadows of that beautiful place. At least I picked a beauty. Things could be worse. I've never told anyone that story." And now, as she talked about it, she felt so shaken.

Jackson's jaw tensed and she could see the pulse throbbing there. His eyes narrowed, and he reached his hand out. "You're not alone. And I promise you that whoever this guy is, he's not going to hurt you again."

"I wish I could believe you."

She laid her hand in Jackson's and as his hand closed around hers, she knew she'd done the right

209

thing telling him. He pulled her close and wrapped his strong arms around her. And when he kissed the top of her head, she told herself to relax, that Jackson was nothing like Joe.

And yet, could she ever truly trust her judgment?

"I'm going to be straight with you, Nina. You are not a fool. You were targeted by what sounds like either a professional or a maniac. I'm not sure but I'm going to find out. I'm falling in love with you. Hear me out, please. It sounds like you probably will have a hard time ever trusting a man again, and I don't blame you. But I'm going to find this guy. I'm going to make sure you can live without having to look back over your shoulder all the time. All I can ask is for you to trust me, if you can."

He was falling in love with her? Her heart ached, knowing she was in love with him and scared she couldn't trust her own judgment. But she wanted to trust him. Had trusted him enough to tell him her crazy past. "I'll trust you," she whispered, because that was all she could get out past the emotions clogging her throat.

"You don't keep all that cash in your house, do you?"

Did she trust him? Yes, she did. "No, I keep it somewhere else."

"And what about security?"

"I've got some cameras and an escape plan."

Jackson cursed under his breath. She'd never heard him curse before.

"You shouldn't have to be going through this. You could move out here to the ranch with me."

She smiled; she couldn't help it. He made her heart happy. "Jackson, I've been safe for three years. I haven't called my police contact in a while, so I think I'll do that. And I was starting to loosen up. That's why I gave your mother the unsigned paintings."

"Maybe you need to take them back. Mom would understand."

"No. I've come to realize I can't live this way forever. I have to face this."

He stared at her. "Okay then, I'll make some calls. I'll get a team of investigators on this. You fill me in on some details and we're going to see what we can find out on this guy when there is unlimited resources."

"I can't ask you to spend a lot of money on me like this."

"That's just it. You didn't ask. This is the right thing to do, and I just happen to have some spare money laying around, just itching to be used for a good cause." And then he leaned in and kissed her.

His kiss stirred feelings inside her she hadn't felt before. So much about this man caused her to feel stronger emotions than she'd ever felt. She wanted to trust them. She was trying to trust him—no, she did trust him. But could she trust herself? Was it even the same thing?

All she knew was as his lips took hers in the tender kiss, she wanted more. It was over before she wanted it to be.

"So, are you still coming to the dinner and charity event next week. It's one of the reasons I've been so busy. There is a lot to it. And because it's also to honor my dad this year I need it to be perfect. My mom usually helps plan it but this year because she has the inn to get ready and because it's the first one since Dad died, I told her I wanted to handle it. It's been more of a job than I anticipated."

"Yes, I'm still planning on coming."

"Great. I'll have hosting duties, but I'd love it if you could be there maybe help Lisa support Mom and maybe save a dance for me."

She could tell what this meant to him. She hadn't been to anything in so very long, but it was very important to them as a family. To him. To Alice. "I'd ride with Lisa and Alice, right?"

"Yes. That way, you'll have friends with you— you'll have more fun."

"You can count on me, I wouldn't change my mind. I want to be there for Alice. And for you."

* * *

Alice was painting one of the bedrooms today. She could have hired all the painting done but she enjoyed it. She hadn't yet made a clear date on what day the inn would open, so she had time to do some of the painting in a few of the rooms. What she couldn't get to, she'd let Seth and his crew do. Seth. He had turned out to be a godsend. He was very talented, and he worked hard and stayed to himself. But he enjoyed when she and Lisa used him to taste test. And she found she enjoyed seeing his reactions to their creations. Lisa was going to be the official chef but Alice did love to bake and to experiment in the kitchen. She'd loved fixing meals for William and her sons. Having Seth enjoy the food she gave him helped that need inside her to make people happy. Soon, she'd enjoy that from the guests at the inn. But it was nice to be able to see Seth's eyes light up. She suspected that he hadn't gotten over his wife's death. It was a connection they shared, though they didn't talk about it. They talked about the inn, the renovations, and occasionally the food.

She and Lisa were set to go shopping for furniture next week, so she wanted the rooms painted before then. She was enjoying herself. And she had decided to paint each of the rooms with a themed color from the paintings that she had gotten from Nina. She was thrilled that her neighbor was such a wonderful artist and had sparked life into Jackson. All these months, she had been worrying about Jackson and the way he had thrown himself into work and kind of disappeared into himself. But ever since he had invited Nina to the cattlemen's dinner and he had seemed excited about it. Low-keyed but excited.

Could there possibly be a blooming relationship there like she was hoping? Could she dare hope it would grow, turn into love? It would be so amazing if Jackson fell for a girl from Star Gazer Island like his dad had.

Although, as she rolled the paint—a soft teal tone, very pale—she wondered at Nina's past. Nina had still kept much of her past to herself. And she felt strongly that Nina was hiding something. She had mentioned to Nina that she should take some of her paintings to the gallery again, that after the morning show had featured them, she was certain many of the gallery owners would love her work. Many of the tourists who came to town loved to buy the beach pictures to take home with them to remember their days here in Corpus Christi or Star Gazer Island; there was a large market for that. But Nina would not do it. She had barely let her buy the ones for the inn. And Alice thought she seemed worried about the morning show feature, asking how wide the viewership was. There had to be a reason for Nina's reluctance. Was it something from her past?

"Alice, I need you," Lisa called. The sound of her steps on the hardwoods told Alice she was coming to her. "Here, you must take a bite of this." Lisa hustled into the room.

The woman was going to make her gain twenty pounds before they opened the inn.

"What is it?"

She was trying all kinds of French cuisine, Italian cuisine, Mediterranean cuisine…and the desserts—oh goodness, the desserts. Thankfully, Seth particularly enjoyed the desserts so that saved her from eating all of it herself.

Lisa was determined to find exactly the right food, testing like a madwoman until they found what she and Lisa believed would be the winning combination of main courses and signature desserts that would set this inn apart from every other restaurant, inn, or B&B in the area. All of their friends were now asking when they would be open. And she had promised before the inn opened they would have an invitation-only luncheon for them all. If they pulled it off, it would put the inn on the map just from the buzz, especially if they could get a review from a food critic. Anticipation was building but they were in no hurry. When it was ready, it would be ready. Lisa was a godsend. The magic ingredient that she had needed.

She let Lisa slip the spoon of creamy chocolate into her mouth. Alice's eyes widened. "Is that chocolate mousse?"

"Somewhat. What do you think?"

"Excellent. Amazing."

Lisa was holding a beautifully presented chocolate delicacy with what tasted like Bavarian cream and something she could not put a name to.

"Lisa, that is so good. I'll take the whole thing, please."

Lisa handed it over. "I've got more. I'm going to run it over to Nina here in a minute and let her try one too. And our man Seth when he gets back from the lumber store. He's going to think he is in heaven. That man does love desserts. Makes you wonder where it goes. Have you noticed the hard abs on that man? And his butt—" She laughed when Alice swatted at her and nearly spit out the mouthful of dessert she'd just taken. "Oh, don't give me that. You know you've noticed too."

"Noticed what?" Jackson asked as he and Riley walked into the room.

Alice's and Lisa's gazes met, and Alice prayed her friend would not embarrass her.

"How good this dessert is." Lisa grinned. "You can take it to Nina for me, and I can keep on baking."

Alice breathed a sigh of relief. And would give Lisa a hug later for getting Jackson to be the delivery man. "That's a great idea. And you can go in there and get you some, and I'll be right there after I put this paintbrush down."

Jackson eyed the dessert in Alice's hand as though he were about to snatch it. Alice smiled, thinking of the time when he'd been ten and he'd taken a whole chocolate pie to the barn and eaten it. He loved chocolate.

Lisa chuckled. "Don't be eyeing my mini chocolate mousse like that, Jackson McIntyre. Follow me to the kitchen. You, too, Riley—when you're ready, of course, and I'll have some waiting for you. But, Jackson, you can't eat yours until you take one to Nina. I really, really need her opinion on this. I value her advice, and I was going to run it over there, but I have more in the oven and can't leave them."

"I'll be happy to do that. I'll take mine, too, and see if she'll let me eat it with her."

Alice and Riley followed them down the hall and Alice almost laughed out loud at Lisa's ploy, it was so blatantly obvious.

In the kitchen, Lisa picked up two dessert bowls of the chocolate mousse and placed them in Jackson's hand. "Here you go. Please bring me back her opinion."

"Yes, ma'am." Jackson smiled then headed out toward the door.

Lisa beat him to it and swung it open, literally pushing big, strong, muscular Jackson out onto the veranda. "Shoo. Hurry. Don't let it get hot." And she shooed him with her hands.

Laughing, Jackson did as she asked.

Alice was certain he didn't mind doing it at all.

Riley grinned at them. "Wow, you two are subtle. I would never in all of my days have gotten a hint that you are trying to fix him and Nina up. I can't believe I haven't met this woman yet. She must be special if you two are trying to fix her and Jackson up. I'm cool with that because the dude needs some fun in his life."

Lisa just crossed her arms and grinned. "I didn't do anything. I'm just making desserts. But I'll tell you this, Riley McIntyre. You need to start thinking about settling down yourself, not thinking about your brother. Now you two go out there and enjoy your dessert and each other. I've got more baking to do." With that, she turned and went to work, mixing a batch of something in a bowl.

"And now you're trying to distract me from what I saw." He laughed as she shot him a grin then turned back to working. Riley took his dessert and followed Alice outside. "She's blunt."

"Yes, she can be." Alice smiled. "But she means

well."

Instead of sitting, they walked down the steps and toward the water. They ate their mousse and stopped at the edge of the property. It was a beautiful afternoon.

"I'm not ready to settle down, Mom."

She touched his arm. Her youngest. Her last baby to rock in a rocking chair. "I know you're not, Riley. I understand. Lisa means well. I'm so glad to have her here."

"I'm glad she's here with you. This is awesome." He held up the bowl. "You picked a winner. I'm surprised she gave up roaming the world. I'd heard she was having a blast away from that dirtbag of a husband of hers."

"You're pretty blunt yourself."

Riley frowned. "He is. It's weird. The woman he left her for was a classmate of mine. You knew that, didn't you? Tabitha Farris."

"Yes, I know. You dated her for a little while, didn't you?"

"Yeah, but it didn't take me long to realize she wanted a ring on her finger and the password to your bank account."

"I'm glad you saw past her. After everything those two have put Lisa through, I'm struggling to harbor any nice thoughts about them. You were very smart.

219

Lisa deserves so much more than she got. And they're terrible. They're still flaunting their affair and love life at Lisa." Oh, had she really said that? "I shouldn't have said that. Please forget you heard that. It was confidential."

"Relax, Mom. I'd never do or say anything to hurt Lisa. And that sounds like Tabitha. Believe me, after we broke up, she did a few things I would never talk about in front of my mother. Anyway, I'm glad Lisa has joined up with you. I wish her well."

"Me too. We are—or were—two of a kind—lost souls searching for our way. She needed me and the inn, and me and the inn needed her." Alice bit her lip and looked out at the ocean. And then she spoke what was on her heart. "And, honestly, Riley, I think maybe something else is going on. But, anyway, I know you're not one to talk, but I do suspect that the river runs deeper through Lisa than any of us realize." She also thought the same thing about Riley, but she didn't say as much; she just hoped that by her saying that he would recognize it himself.

"Maybe so, but the only thing I can say is that Lisa knows her way around good food. This is delicious. Are y'all going to serve this at the inn?"

"I believe we are. And it might be the winner of our signature dish. It is wonderful. I think it's something everyone would love. Kids and adults alike."

"I think so, too. Anyway, all I can say is I need a gigantic bowl of it, so if you can put an order in for me, just tell her to make it in a gallon bowl, box it up, and I'll be by to pick it up."

She laughed and patted his washboard abs. "I don't think those stomach muscles you have there come from eating gallons of chocolate mousse, so I think you're just teasing."

"Hey, Mom, that right there comes from hard work. Seriously, Mom, I really have a feeling that when you get this inn going, it's going to be a huge success. You're going to have a lot of our cattle-ranching friends come to the coast more often. This place is going to be beautiful. And to think, you and Dad met here. I think this is a really cool idea. I have to admit that, at first, I couldn't imagine you doing this. Couldn't imagine you moving off the ranch. But Mom…" He paused to look at her; his pale-honey eyes simmered with emotion. "You look good. Dad would be so proud of you. And you look happier than you've looked in a long time. Are you?"

Tears welled in Alice's eyes. She reached out and wrapped an arm around his waist, then leaned her head against his shoulder. "I feel happier, Riley. I really,

really do. It's just something I needed to do, and I'm so glad you understand."

He kissed the top of her head. "I do. And I'm happy for you."

CHAPTER NINETEEN

The evening of the cattle sale and charity auction, Nina put on her little red cocktail dress, having asked Alice what was appropriate to wear to the cattleman's dinner. She was not a cattle person or a rancher lady and had no idea of what wealthy cattle owners and their wives and counterparts wore to such functions. But Alice had assured her that her red dress was perfect, that it wasn't a black-tie event—which Alice said she had attended more of those in her lifetime than she ever wanted to attend again. Therefore, this was dressy but not over the top. It was to be fun and enjoyable, and her sons would not enjoy anything for very long if it required them to wear a suit. The sale dinner that they did was a little more laid-back and enjoyable.

Jackson had assured her of the same things yesterday when he'd come over with the rich, decadent chocolate mousse Lisa had sent him to deliver. They'd had coffee and talked some, and he'd said he had used bringing Riley by to see the inn as an excuse to check on her. That had pleased Nina. It felt nice to feel like someone cared.

So now, wearing her red dress and after giving Buttercup a big hug and a kiss on the top of her head before putting her back in her kennel, she grabbed her small purse with only her phone and her lip gloss and headed outside to meet Lisa and Alice. The limousine pulled into the inn's circle drive just as she started across the lawn toward them, wobbling on the heels she'd bought just for tonight. She hadn't dressed up like this since she'd gone into hiding, and it felt good. In her life before, at gallery showings, she'd enjoyed dressing up. Though she hadn't really missed the gatherings that much, it was nice to dress up sometimes. And she couldn't help wondering whether Jackson would think she looked nice.

He had also gone through her house, making sure she had what she needed to be safe. Just as he'd done for his mother when he'd learned she was opening the inn. She now had twenty-four-hour surveillance that he'd insisted on. He'd put it in his name because she hadn't been able to go that far on her security, not wanting to give her name or credit card information. He'd also hired what seemed like an army to search for Joe—whatever his actual name was, no one knew at this point. She'd called the cop she was in contact with and he'd told her that Joe had gone dark, meaning nothing was turning up on him at all. She hoped she was dark, and that nothing was showing up on her either.

The cop, Tim, had also told her that the truth was, with the limited resources the department had, that her case was now on the back burner. Because she was out of sight and out of mind—and safe, it seemed—they had moved on to more pressing cases. But to keep doing what she was doing.

And that was the problem. She didn't always want to keep hiding. She wanted her normal life back. And Jackson was determined to give that to her. He had resources, and if this guy was alive, his people would find him. Money talked.

"See there," Lisa teased, her eyes sparkling. "You are teetering across that yard like you've had several mimosas today."

She laughed as she stepped onto the driveway. "I haven't, I promise. I just haven't worn heels in a long time."

Lisa gaped wide eyed at her. "You're serious?"

She laughed. "I've enjoyed being a flip-flop girl."

"Me too," Alice agreed. "I know I'll bring some low heels out for a few events, but my day for shoes with those three- or four-inch heels are long over."

Lisa shot a well-shaped leg out from beneath her black sheath dress that looked sleek and wonderful on her. "I love heels and have no plans to downsize. My fifty-fourth birthday is coming up in two months. I may dress up and wear a hot pair of red four-inch Louboutin. These are only three inch but I love them. And they are excellent dancing shoes."

The limo driver opened the door for them and they all climbed inside.

"So how are you and Jackson getting along?" Alice asked as soon as they were inside the limo.

She had been avoiding them some this week because she'd been spending time with Jackson, and she didn't want to answer questions about them.

Lisa hitched a brow. "We have seen him around a lot this week. Just so you realize we might be a few years older than you, but we are not blind."

She smiled at that. "I know. It's just a bit awkward talking about him with his mother and her best friend."

"I'm sure it is." Alice sighed. "But we are your friends too. And we want the best for both of you."

"I'm just making sure you're having the time of your life tonight. You have on that gorgeous red dress and those sweet shoes and a gorgeous cowboy waiting for you. You need to dance the night away. You have been hiding in that house of yours for too long. He's a gorgeous guy. One of the good cowboys and you shouldn't let him get away."

She drew in a shaky breath. She agreed with everything Lisa said. "You two better not start matchmaking. I'm not at all comfortable with any of this. I haven't dated in three years."

"It's high time you started. At your age, and after what you went through, it's time. You need to find out what life with a good man is like. And I might be partial to my son, but like Lisa said, he is one of the good guys."

They had no idea how good he was. After all the care he'd taken this week with her safety in mind and now the private investigators he had hunting for "Joe," she no longer questioned trusting him. She did trust him.

"And I believe me buying the inn right next to you was a godsend. You're perfect for Jackson."

And if she hadn't already been nervous about going to this party, she was now.

* * *

Jackson wore his Western black suit jacket and his

starched jeans with his black dress boots, and waited by the large tent that they always set up to hold this yearly sale in. The cattle sale had happened earlier and now everyone was here to enjoy great food, networking, and a silent auction that would benefit several communities that had suffered damage from a tornado recently. And they were here to honor his dad.

They hadn't had the sale last year because his dad's accident happened a few months prior to the scheduled sale. That had meant that everyone had shown up this year to support them in continuing their dad's legacy. His heart was full with all the well wishes and he knew it was time for him to come to terms with his dad's death.

Now, as he stood in his father's place to welcome their guests, he felt the weight of stepping into his father's boots. It wasn't something he'd ever planned to happen this soon, but for his family, he was doing it. A black SUV pulled up and his brother Dallas climbed out.

Jackson was glad to see him. He'd said he was going to try to make it and probably had to book a private jet to fly him in from a bull riding event. Dallas was good, but it was easy to see as he limped slightly that his career choice was wearing on him. As the next to the oldest, Dallas knew as well as everyone that bull riders were pro athletes and their careers had shelf lives. Dallas had peaked already, being a two-time NFR champion. It had been four years ago, and his standings were dropping every year. But he'd managed to hang on and was still one of the top riders in the circuit.

"You made it." Jackson stepped forward and engulfed Dallas in a hug. It had been a few weeks and tonight was hard. It just was. He had to come to grips with the loss of his dad and move forward. Dallas had talked him off the ledge several times since the accident, always reminding Jackson that their dad was strong-willed and had made the choice to cross that river on his own. It was all true but that didn't stop the nightmares or keep him from feeling the heavy load of guilt.

Dallas hugged him tight then stepped back. "I told you I'd get here. Can't stay too long but I had to come for the night. I have a date with a really ugly bull tomorrow, so I'll be flying out after breakfast."

"Mom will be glad you came. She should be driving up any minute. Her, Lisa, and Nina."

Dallas's lip curved. "Nina, the neighbor you keep mentioning."

"Yes."

"Something's going on between you two. You don't normally talk about a woman but the last two times I've called, you have mentioned her."

"Hey, she's Mom's neighbor. I see her when I'm over there, and she went riding a couple of times." He had mentioned that he'd shown her the swimming hole.

"And you have never taken a woman out there."

He smiled. There was no hiding it anyway. "You're right. I'm not going to deny it."

He spotted his mother's limousine turn in to the circle drive. They always had the same driver for their mom because the driver was also one of the best bodyguards in the business and they didn't have to worry about their mom being unsafe. And he didn't have to worry about Nina being unsafe. He'd made a lot of headway on finding this "Joe Jerk" that he hadn't told her about. He would later. Tonight, he wanted her to have fun. She'd been under a lot of stress, though he hadn't realized it until she'd trusted him with her past. And he didn't want her worrying about what was about to happen. There would be time enough for that later.

The limo pulled to a stop at the designated spot, and someone walked up and asked him a question at that exact moment. He answered their question as quickly as possible, as the greeter stepped up and opened the door. His mom got out; Lisa got out behind her. And then, just as he was heading in that direction, a silver high heel came out of the limousine, followed by a long leg and Nina in a pretty red dress that fit her perfectly, flared out just around her hip. His heart kicked up and his pulse raced. He'd told her he was falling in love with her, but he'd lied. He was in love with her, and the idea that she'd been afraid of this guy stalking her made him sick. But it was weird to know that if she hadn't been hiding out, he probably would have never met her.

He smiled at her now, wanting to take her in his arms, wanting to tell her his true feelings, but he needed to make sure she was safe first. She hadn't said anything about his declaration that day at the pond. But he hadn't pressed her because he knew it wasn't the right time. She had too much on her mind, and he didn't want her to be confused. He wanted her to feel completely safe. When she shifted her gaze in his direction and caught sight of him, his heart warmed when he saw a receptive flare in her eyes. It looked like she was glad to see him too.

"Welcome, ladies. Glad to see you, Lisa and Mom. You two are looking beautiful tonight." He kissed his mother's cheek.

"Thank you." She hugged him. "It's going to be a good night. Your dad would be proud of you. And Dallas, you made it." She threw her arms around Dallas as he stepped up for his hug. "I was so hoping you would make it."

"I wouldn't miss it, Mother."

She cupped his cheek. "His boys…all of you will be here. He's smiling right now, I'm sure."

Jackson saw the emotion in her eyes. "Are you okay?"

She nodded, looking from Dallas to him. "I'm doing good. Just a bit emotional. It will be good to see old friends. He did love this event every year."

"Yes, he did." He turned and gave Lisa a hug as she had been waiting for them to greet their mother. "Lisa, I'm glad you could come too." He hugged her and whispered, "Thanks for being here for Mom."

She patted his shoulder and that was enough to let him know no thanks were necessary. "What are friends for but to be there for each other," she said quietly. Then she smiled broadly. "Thank you for the invite. And may I say, you are looking as handsome as ever." She hitched her head toward Nina. "What about Nina?"

He smiled broadly, having saved the best for last. "Nina, you are lovely. I'm glad you came too."

"I'm glad to be here. I wouldn't have missed it for the world after you told me it was to honor your father."

He'd told her about how much his dad had loved this event and that it would mean a lot to his mother. "It'll be a good night. Here, let me introduce you to Dallas."

Dallas held out his hand and grinned. "It's nice to meet you. I hear only good things about you."

She blushed. "Really? It's nice to meet you."

Jackson still had a lot of people to greet. "Let's get these ladies to their table." He held his arm out; Nina slipped her arm through his, and Dallas held his arms out for their mom and for Lisa.

His mother smiled over her shoulder at him, and he knew without a doubt that she had hopes for him and Nina.

Lisa looked over her shoulder at him, too. "I hope you know every cowboy in this place is going to come try to get a dance with Nina."

He chuckled. "I might not be the sharpest tool in the toolshed, but I'm not stupid." He leaned in to Nina. "I'm going to hope you'll save me a dance or two. Of course, if you want to dance with anybody, that's your choice. I'll take what I can get. I do have some master of ceremony duties I have to take care of, but then I'm going to be standing in line with everyone else."

She blushed. "I hope so."

They reached the table, and his mom and Lisa set their wraps on the back of their seats.

He turned so his and Nina's conversation was more private. "I'm hoping you have a good time tonight. I'm planning to be by your side as much as possible, if you don't mind."

Her expression was soft, and her eyes searched his. "I'd like that."

He smiled, and then he brushed his lips across hers. "You just made my night."

He wanted to spend the rest of his life with her, but he didn't want to run her off by moving too fast.

He held the seat out for her, and she sat down beside his mom. She and Lisa were watching him with approving smiles. He just smiled. "Enjoy yourselves. I'll be back. I have a party to get started first."

And the sooner this party started, the sooner he would get to dance with Nina.

CHAPTER TWENTY

Nina was having a great time. She realized that, in hiding out like she had been doing, there were things she had given up. Like just the excitement of dressing up and going to a party; it didn't even have to be a fancy party, just something simple—visiting with people and enjoying casual chatting. Of course, she had Alice and Lisa introducing her to everyone in the room, and she did feel a bit guilty that her actual name wasn't being used. Hopefully, one day soon she could be truthful with Alice and Lisa, but she didn't want them knowing who she was right now. Maybe she'd read too much on stalkers, and maybe she was being paranoid, but she didn't want to endanger these two lovely ladies by giving them information that would put them in a situation of having to lie about her if "Joe" ever came around asking questions.

It would be better if they truly didn't know anything. She had been praying that Jackson and the investigators he'd hired might actually find the guy, but she knew it would take time.

So tonight, she was having a really good time. And she loved watching Jackson when he gave the opening speech, talking about his father and how much he'd loved hosting the event and that everyone always came out to buy the cattle but also to support the good cause the auction helped out every year. She found herself wishing she'd known William McIntyre. She heard many stories about him as she stood by Alice's side over the next hour. Everyone wanted to come by to talk to her and reminisce, and many of them offered their well wishes for the inn.

Many of the ladies had seen the morning show and asked Alice about the artwork. Alice pointed to Nina and let them know she had painted the pieces. When Alice had first told her about the show, Nina's heart dropped to her feet, realizing her work had been on television. Realizing that someone could recognize it… Then she'd assured herself it had just been local news—not national—and the odds were low that Joe would have seen the show. But tonight it was hard talking about her artwork and not telling the truth about it. She got out of each conversation as quickly as possible, turning the conversation back to the inn, Alice or Lisa.

That wasn't too hard to do since everyone was glad to see them out and about after their ordeals. Lisa amazed her as she entertained people with stories of her travels. She had an effervescence and completely enthralling personality that captivated people. Alice was more low-key but gracious and drew people to her. And as Nina had often thought along the way and now saw people gravitating to the two ladies, she believed even more that the Star Gazer Inn was destined to become a sought-after luncheon spot and event destination. These two were gold together and knowing the hardships they'd both been through made it more sweet to watch the joy on their faces tonight.

When Jackson crossed the room toward her, Nina could not look away from him. He had her attention from the moment their gazes connected. The man was handsome beyond description and he looked so perfect. Her heart pounded as he got close and held his hand out to her.

"Can you come with me for a little while? I've abandoned you long enough."

"Yes, please go enjoy yourself." Alice gave her a gentle push. "We can take care of ourselves."

She laughed. "Yes, ma'am."

Her hand was tingling in Jackson's as, smiling, he led her across the room and through the side opening of the gorgeously decorated tent. From the inside of that tent, you would never guess from all the crystal and silver and floor arrangements and the beautiful chandeliers hanging from the ceilings that they weren't at the fanciest hotel in the country. But they walked out onto the flagstone patios set up, where lights were strung out and seating was grouped around firepits. He introduced her to a few people but never truly stopped as he led the way to one of the seating arrangements at the far end of the patio.

Once there, he faced her. "I had to get you out here all to myself for a little while."

"Oh really. And why would that be?" She leaned into him.

The music could be heard well from this spot and, to her surprise, he slipped his arm around her, tugged her close, and started slow dancing. It was so unexpected. But so wonderful.

"I'm thinking this dance would be better if it was out under the stars. Can't do that inside of the tent," he said close to her ear.

She relaxed, glad to be right where she was. "Yes, you did tell me that."

"And I'm not one to not carry out my promises. Besides, I've been looking forward to this dance all evening. You are stunning."

She looked into his eyes. "Thank you. I've really enjoyed myself."

Their faces were close, and she was now imagining kisses from him. She told herself not to get carried away, but she couldn't help it.

They just swayed to the music. She rested her cheek against his chest and let the beauty of the moment hold her in place. After all the horrible mistakes, terrible men—here in Jackson's arms, the soft light of hope entered her heart.

"I've heard a lot of people say positive things about Mom's inn, and they're also talking about your art. They're excited about seeing your paintings. I'm hoping soon you'll be able to start letting people know who you are. And you can start signing them again."

Her breath caught in her chest. "No. I have my reasons. I worry about Joe seeing that show, though I keep telling myself it was local and the chances are low that he would have seen it."

He paused their slow dancing. "I thought about that too and you're right, the chances of him seeing that local show is small. And I wasn't going to mention this yet, but we have some leads we're checking out. Just so you know."

She was trying to concentrate on his words, and not the fact that she was in his arms, with one hand resting on his heart and the other hand in his hand as he held her close with one large hand spread across her back. It would be so easy to relax into him. So easy not to want to hear what he was saying. "They've found him?"

The fear that had been in the shadows of her life over the last three years settled like hot lava in the pit of her stomach. She'd always worried he might be watching newspapers for something about her art and be able to find her. Or television. Or social media. He'd scared her so badly and no one had found him until now. If they stirred him up, somehow tipped him off where she was...she'd have to leave. She had begun to love her life here and she didn't want anything to intrude on it. The last thing she ever wanted to do was to run again. Especially now that she had Alice, Lisa, and Jackson.

"Nina, I see your mind working. You're worrying. Please don't. This is why I didn't want to tell you tonight. But now that you know, understand that nothing is going to happen to you. I have surveillance on you at all times. If he were to show up here, we would nab him immediately. Come on now, look at me," he said gently.

She lifted worried eyes to his, needing to feel his strength.

He smiled. "Think about how it will be to resume

your life. To be able to show your work with your name on it. Your work is beautiful. Beautiful like you. There is a quietness to it but a vibrant beauty to it also that calls out to a person. It needs to be shown, not hidden in a back room."

She forgot everything but him in that moment. "What a nice thing to say."

"It's the truth. Ever since I met you, I've been intrigued by you. You are reserved and quiet, but I'm pretty sure that that spunky person I glimpse sparkling in your eyes sometimes is the real Nina and that you are tired of being hidden."

His words hit home like darts to a target board. "That's how you think of me?" It was as if he had looked into her eyes and seen everything she was trying to hide.

"Yes. And I want to find this guy and set you free."

Time ticked between them as they stared at each other. As a new slow song started up, he began moving slowly to the music again. It helped her relax as his arms tightened around her, sturdy and secure. Safe.

She felt drawn to him and wanted this with all of her heart. "I want to be free of the past so I can look toward the future."

"And I'm hoping that will include me."

And then he lowered his lips and covered hers

with his. Her breath caught at the touch of his warm lips, and his hand tugged her slightly closer, to where she had no choice but to relax into his body and feel his embrace tighten around her. This kiss was stronger than the kiss they'd shared at the swimming hole. It was deeper and drew her in and took her breath away.

All she could think about was Jackson and his kiss.

CHAPTER TWENTY-ONE

Jackson lost all his ability to think straight as he kissed Nina. He had never been afraid to go after what he wanted but now, holding Nina, he knew he'd never wanted anything in his life like he wanted her. He'd kissed her lightly at the swimming pond and it had been a testing of the waters and she'd kissed him back. But tonight, he kissed her with all the emotion she drew from him. He'd never been attracted to anyone or wanted anyone more than he wanted Nina—heart, body, and soul. And when she softened against him, responding with such sweetness, such welcome, it was as if the sun had come out on his world. For the first time in his life, he knew exactly what his future was going to be.

It was crazy thinking on his part. She had too much on her mind right now and he was not going to pressure her. He was going to take this moment and cherish it, find the creep who was causing her all this grief and then, afterward, there would be time to be more than her friend. But right now, she needed a friend with benefits…one with deep pockets and a debt to settle with this guy who had her scared and on the run.

Now that he'd come to his senses, he pulled back and looked into her dazed eyes and her kiss-swollen lips. "I hope I didn't just scare you to death with that kiss. Look, I have deep feelings for you, but you don't need all of that right now. You need a friend who can help you get the past in the past. That's me. So, while I loved everything about that kiss, I don't think you need any more pressure on you. So it won't happen again. Not until we set you free from all this worry hanging over you. Okay?"

She moistened her lips. "I am a bit confused by all of this."

"I have a tendency to go after what I want. So, it was a natural thing for me to move too fast. I'm sorry for rushing you. Let's go rejoin the party so I won't misbehave anymore, and you can feel comfortable again."

He took her hand, and they walked back inside.

Riley strode toward them the minute they entered the large tent. Riley was lean, tall, and had an easier face to get along with than Jackson. Riley's personality drew women. They chased after him, and he enjoyed it. He was outgoing, passionate about causes, and had a thriving social life. As he walked toward them, women's heads turned and followed his every step.

Jackson smiled as he approached them. He didn't think Nina had met him yet and that was probably the reason Riley was coming over. He was curious about the woman they all knew had captured Jackson's attention.

"Hi, I'm Riley," he said before Jackson could introduce him. He held his hand out to Nina.

He was glad to have Riley to take over the conversation for now, so it would take the edge off their kissing encounter. Jackson was going to move slower or he might scare her off.

"I'm glad to meet you, Riley."

* * *

Nina shook Riley's hand. Her thoughts were muddled from Jackson's kiss—there was no denying that she had wanted that kiss. But he was right; they did not need that right now.

She berated herself for having so easily fallen into

romance mode. Had she not learned anything through her horrible marriage and then being totally, completely humiliated and conned by Joe in that rebound relationship gone terrible? Had she not even learned to take things slow? Sure, she hadn't dated for three years, that was fairly cautious, but she'd become a weak ball of clay at his kiss. This amazing kiss that left her heart both confused but hopeful.

Fighting down the turmoil inside her, she smiled at Riley and hoped he couldn't see the barrage of emotions going on behind her eyes. But Riley McIntyre had a devilish look in his eyes. He and Jackson looked like brothers, as did Dallas and Tucker, but this younger version of the McIntyre man was nothing like his reserved older brother. Riley was gorgeous and he knew it. But as he crooked a smile at her that told the world that he enjoyed a good time and loved life, she could not help but like him. Not that Jackson didn't love life, but he had more on his shoulders than Riley and it showed.

"Jackson didn't tell me that Mom's neighbor was beautiful. I'd have dropped by sooner." He gave a warm smile then shifted his gaze to Jackson.

Clearly, he was teasing his brother as much as he was teasing her. He was trying to make his older brother jealous. That was his ploy. Not comfortable at all with that, she tried to remain calm as she tugged her fingers from his. "I've seen you dancing out there. It's a wonder your boots are not on fire."

He tucked his fingers in the pocket of his jeans. "I know. It's terrible, isn't it? I can't help myself when the music starts—I've got the rhythm in me. Now Jackson there…he's got some rhythm but you kind of have to force him to get out there. Me, my foot starts tapping and next thing you know, I'm on the dance floor. If I didn't have a girl on my arm, I'd probably be out there dancing by myself. Speaking of, do you hear that? It's starting back up, and I need a partner." He held out his hand to her.

She was so tempted. But she looked at Jackson. He laughed, and she relaxed just a bit. For a moment there, she had visions of her ex growing angry when anyone showed her attention. He had been so jealous and accused her of so many horrible things, and in the end, he was the one doing all the horrible things.

"Go on," Jackson urged. "Dance with Riley if you want. My brother is a flirt, and he does know how to dance. And he's right. I like slow dances and that dance music isn't slow."

"Okay then, but I have to warn you I'm not a great dancer."

"I love to teach a woman how to dance." And with that, Riley took her hand and swung her out on the dancefloor.

She immediately stepped on his toes but he just grinned and twirled her around. She twirled so much she almost got dizzy. She hadn't laughed so much in a long time. Riley was an amazing Western dancer; he spun her and slung her and drew her in and they twirled around together. It was the most active dance she'd ever had. She wasn't even sure whether it was a waltz or a swing dance or a fast-paced two-step; it was just fun. And when he dipped her suddenly, holding her horizontal to the dance floor for a long moment, he looked down into her eyes and winked.

"My brother is about to have a coronary over there." Then he'd laughed and set her back on her feet before twirling her around some more.

She had to admit the idea that Jackson could possibly be jealous was intriguing, despite her horrible experience with overblown jealousy from her ex. But with Jackson, she would have felt jealous if he were dancing like this with anyone. It was a new feeling for her. But this was nothing like what she'd been through with her ex and she knew it. This was just her admitting that she cared for Jackson and she couldn't bear to think of him with someone else.

By the end of the evening, she was exhausted. She had long ago lost the high heels. And she had enjoyed a couple of slower dances with Jackson, inside the tent and without the kissing. They had not gone back outside under the stars, and they had not kissed again at all. He hadn't been kidding when he'd said he wasn't going to scare her off.

And that was a good thing. She needed to keep her mind on being cautious in every aspect of her life. As she and Alice and Lisa climbed back into their limo around eleven, she felt like Cinderella. It had been a lovely evening, and she was getting home in plenty of time before her carriage turned into a pumpkin. And yet she felt like tomorrow she would go back to the real world and hopefully have her head on straight and she could think clearly once more.

CHAPTER TWENTY-TWO

Riley stared around the room at his older brothers. Dallas was flying out in less than thirty minutes, and he'd wanted to run his idea by them.

So, he just had to deal with Dallas, Tucker, and Jackson. They looked at him as though he'd lost his mind. "Take me serious, okay? Stop looking at me like that. This is a good idea."

Jackson's brows knitted over skeptical eyes, telling Riley without words what he thought of his idea. And he wasn't taking it seriously. He shot a glare at Tucker and then hoped Dallas might back him but was afraid he'd get the same sentiment from him as his other brothers.

Anger knotted in his gut. Riley spun on his heel

and stomped to the fireplace, trying to calm down. They had to get it. He wasn't backing down and throwing a fit was not the answer. "It sounds silly but it's not. It's a good idea."

"So let me get this straight," Jackson said. "You want to put a fancy camping area out on our coastal ranch land. Glamping? Is that what you called it?"

"Yeah, glamping. It's a hot trend and it's a money maker." Not that it was going to make them another billion or even a million, but it was profitable. He'd run the numbers. "I want to do it, and all I'm doing is coming and getting everybody's thoughts on the process. But I have as much right to put it out there as anybody. So, you might think I'm crazy, but I think it's going to be a big hit. Besides, we've got enough land—it won't hurt for me to do that."

Dallas chuckled. "I'm actually curious about it. Women come to these glamping campsites?"

"And get *massages*?" Tucker asked.

Riley laughed, relief that they hadn't outright laughed at him. "Yeah. Women who don't want to rough it but want to get out in the open space with their girlfriends."

Jackson looked confused. "So they have spa days?"

"I know it sounds a little bit outrageous, but yes, if they want spa days, they can have spa days. It's just a

getaway for them to be close to nature in a safe
environment with other like-minded ladies. Look, a lot
of these ladies have fancy little travel trailers, some
vintage and painted all wild and cool. They come out
there and they have a good time and they get fancy
food. Some have cooking classes with celebrity chefs.
They do all kinds of stuff. They get that gunk on their
face like Mom used to do sometimes—that green stuff,
you know? And they relax and they get their
fingernails done and toenails done. And they can get a
massage too. There are all kinds of things to offer. The
sky is the limit. It's pretty cool. I'm just kind of
pumped ever since I started thinking about it and
researching them. You know, I told you a little bit
about it before, but you didn't take me seriously. Now
I'm totally serious."

Dallas leaned back in his chair grinning. "Heck, I
say go for it."

Jackson nodded agreement. "I'm not going to say
no, just because I don't understand it doesn't mean I
have the right to tell you not to do it."

"And you're right," Tucker agreed, "We've got
the land."

"So go for it," Jackson said. "Do what you want to
with it. I'm kind of curious to see what it looks like
when you're done. But you can't get it started and then
just leave it."

Riley did not like him saying that. "Jackson, have you ever known me to start something and then not finish it?"

"No. Forget I said that. I don't even know why I did say it."

"You said it because it's something Dad would've said. And the truth is, as much as Dad liked to explore new ideas, this is one I have no doubt he would've said no too. I would've had to go out on my own and push if I had wanted to go for it. But I think Mom will really like it."

Jackson gave him a look that was a mirror of how Riley felt. "I think so too. It fits right up there with her inn and that pink monstrosity she bought and put in the library room."

They all laughed about that horrible piece of furniture because it *was* awful, in their minds. But she loved it.

"Maybe so, but like that inn, it's going to be a hit. Mark my words, big brothers." He thought of his mother. "She looked good last night. She's having a blast working on that inn. She seems more content."

They all sobered and nodded their heads in agreement thinking about their mom.

Jackson looked thoughtful. "Yeah. A few days ago, I stopped by and she was sitting on the patio area, humming as she worked on some projections for the inn. She said her contractor had agreed to stay on and build her a gazebo for weddings, and she was working on pricing. He's already redone the bathrooms and they're really fancy now. That made her happy. She just looks happier about everything."

Riley's heart squeezed. He'd hated the idea of her opening the inn and moving off the ranch, and he'd only been to see her a very few times . He needed to fix that. "You were right. We needed to support her in this. I'm glad she's doing better. I've got to go by and see her more. I miss coming in here and giving her a hug every morning, but I get it now."

Dallas sighed. "Moving on without Dad has been hard on all of us. But for her... I can't imagine if I ever loved someone like she did Dad—it would tear my heart out. Makes me take a good hard look at marrying. I'm not good with giving things up. Giving up someone I gave my heart to doesn't sound like something I'd want to do."

"She's made the right move," Tucker said.

Jackson walked over to the window overlooking the flowers in the garden that his mother always tended before. Now one of their ranch hands took care of them and it wasn't the same. "You're all speaking truth there. She's been forced to look at a future that works for her now, not the one she and Dad had envisioned. And she's doing that. I admire the heck out of her for choosing to reach for something unexpected that gives her a sense of accomplishment at the end of the day. And helps fill the void. She loved and she lost but she'd be the first to tell us she wouldn't trade anything for the years she had loving Dad." He turned back to them. "Watching her makes me more sure that I want to know that kind of love. Not miss it because I was too set in my ways or too afraid of the pain it could cost me down the road. Me, I haven't gotten used to not seeing Dad every morning and I never will. Him telling us his plans for the day or just joining us on the cattle drive or a branding. And now having to get used to him not being in this big house and Mom not being here either, it just doesn't seem right. And yet seeing her at the inn feels right."

"She was the heart of this monster of a house," Dallas said.

"Yes, she was." Tucker stood and started pacing.

The house was huge. Their dad had built it and it had gotten out of hand. But when they were growing up, they'd gotten used to it. Now it was mostly Jackson and their housekeeper, Rose, here.

Riley stayed at the camp house most of the time, preferring to be able to walk out onto the back porch and watch the deer drinking out of the creek. Jackson was the one who kept the books for the ranch and was chained to the desk, pretty much. That was not for him.

Funny, no one had ever asked Jackson whether that was his preference. It was just assumed. "Jack, you ever thinking about moving out of here? Maybe building you a smaller place? I like life at the camp house, having some privacy from all you knuckleheads when everyone is in town. But it's just nice to have my own place."

His brothers laughed. Growing up together, they sometimes wanted space. Brothers didn't always get along. The camp house had always been a place to get away to; Riley had settled in and never left a couple of years ago.

Jackson's eyes narrowed. "Growing up, we didn't have it bad here in this big house. There's plenty of space, for sure. There's a lot of people who would feel blessed with a rambling house like this. I'm still trying to figure out what I'm going to do. One minute, I feel trapped here and the next, I hate the idea of leaving. It's home. There's always a place for everyone to come. Who knows? Maybe one day we'll all have families like Mom is hoping and we'll gather here. Looking at us right now, that is hard to imagine. None of y'all seem anywhere near ready to settle down. Dallas basically said he might never marry. Tucker didn't say much at all and everyone can tell you're not ready, Riley."

He shrugged, unable to deny it. "All I know is

finding a wife is not what's eating up my thoughts right now." Riley pinned Jackson with a curious stare. "What about you and Nina? You've been spending a lot of time seeing her. And you know good and well you were jealous last night every time I stole her away from you."

Jackson might not have even realized the way his expression brightened just at the very mention of the pretty lady's name. His brother needed to get married. He was the oldest brother. Maybe if he would get married and have some babies, he would seem happier. Jackson hadn't been in the best of moods since their daddy died. Course, Riley understood. They all did. When the accident happened, he had been too far back to see what a fool move their dad made riding off into the river with no one close enough to help if he got into trouble. Why he'd done it, they'd never know. Jackson had seen it all, but been unable to get to him. Jackson had only one shot at saving him and that was with his rope, but his rope had been too short. Riley would never forget the look in Jackson's eyes when they'd reached him. They'd had to haul him off his horse before he dove in and went after Dad.

"You need to date that lady. She suits you."

"I agree," Dallas said, his gaze meeting Riley's.

"I like her. But, look, it's not as easy as it sounds. She holds back and has good reasons. She's been through hell and back, and has some ongoing trouble from her past I'm helping with now."

Tucker cocked his head to one side. "What?"

"I'm not at liberty to divulge that at the moment. But believe me, I'm not giving up. I've been thinking about my life this last little while. And I don't want to be by myself. I'm thinking about settling down and she's special."

Dallas stood. "Well, I'll be. You're going for the full ride."

Jackson chuckled. "Yup. I'm going to hang in there for the full eight seconds and longer. I've never been much of a bull rider—that's your avenue of expertise, Dallas. But on this, I'm going to see it through."

"Good for you," Tucker said.

Riley grinned. "Now that sounds like the Jackson I know." He headed toward the door. "You hang in there and marry your lady. I've got glamping plans to make." And with that, he headed out the door. He turned back. "Dallas, you take care of yourself. Tuck, fair warning I'm going to win my money back from you at the pool table tomorrow night. And Jackson, I don't want to pry, and I don't know what's going on with Nina's past, but if you need me for anything, all you have to do is ask."

His brothers had come through for him. They'd

had his back in this and it felt good knowing he had their support in taking a risk and starting up something different. It made him all the more determined not to fail.

Tucker was hard to read and content to ride the ranch doing what they all loved.

Dallas was one of the best bull riders in the world, but he couldn't ride bulls forever. Riley hoped he gave it up before he got himself hurt. But that wasn't a decision he could make. A man had to do what a man had to do, and only Dallas could know when to let it go.

Jackson had good things going on and Riley was thrilled. He was just a little worried about the seriousness of Jackson's tone when he'd said some ongoing trouble from Nina's past was holding them back. He hoped it wasn't something dangerous.

Sometimes he saw life like a bowl of cherries, and he might enjoy it a bit too much. But that didn't mean he was clueless, and hopefully his brothers knew he also had their backs if they needed him.

* * *

Nina held a cup of coffee in her hand as the morning sunlight streamed through the windows and landed on the canvas she was working on. "What do you think,

259

Buttercup? Just a little something that I'm working on."

Buttercup cocked her little head to the side, her blue eyes contemplating the painting.

Nina almost laughed, expecting the dog to answer at any moment, she looked so serious. "Okay, okay. I get that it needs something more." It needed her head to be in the game, but it wasn't. After last night, she had lain in bed staring up at the shadows in her ceiling, thinking about that kiss. And then thinking about Joe and how she had fallen and been so gullible for his charms. And then…she shook herself. Jackson wasn't like that. He was protecting her.

She wasn't going to think about any of that right now. Thinking about her involvement with Joe was unhealthy for her. It caused her to have flashbacks sometimes and to peer into shadows and worry that he was going to somehow show up, and she didn't need to think like that. She was learning to move forward and not live in fear. Jackson was helping her be able to do that.

She'd looked out the window last night and spotted a car down the road. He'd said he had someone watching her. It felt creepy but also comforting. Someone was watching over her, and Joe wasn't going to come in and threaten her. Or tear her place up or stalk her anymore. Eventually Jackson was going to find him, and they would arrest him. She hoped.

At the tap on her back door, she jumped and Buttercup scrambled up, barking as if they were being invaded. She spun toward the back door, fear racing through her and coffee sloshing out of her coffee cup onto her feet.

Jackson stood at the glass door, frowning.

Relief washed over her. Breathing hard, she waved and forced a smile and hoped that she didn't look completely frightened to him. She set her coffee mug down, grabbed a towel, and quickly wiped the floor. Then she hurried to the door, praying that she had her composure together by the time she opened the door. "Jackson, what are you doing here?" She hadn't meant to sound accusatory. She was actually very glad to see him.

"I came by to talk. Want to walk on the beach?"

"Sure. Would you like a cup of coffee? I have a fresh pot."

"That would be good."

She crossed to the coffee carafe, feeling jittery. *What did he need to talk to her about?* She pulled out a gray mug and handed it to him full of black brew. She grabbed her own cup, a red one, and walked back out to join him. She felt a thrill at the sudden picture of him standing there like that in the sunlight, watching her move toward him. No, she wasn't going to let herself go there. She wanted to almost believe she was walking toward her future as she walked toward him. Them together, married, and her house being their beach cottage and his house being their home. And them having the best of both worlds.

She was losing it.

Walking past him, she smiled over her shoulder. "Ready to walk out to the water?"

He removed his hat and hung it on the corner of the Adirondack chair, and then tugged a pair of sunshades out of his pocket and put them on. They walked together across the sand. Buttercup trotted beside them, thrilled to be heading for a walk on the beach.

"It hasn't taken my dog long to fall in love with the water. She knows that when I take a few steps off the porch we are going to the water and she loves it."

"That's good. She seems settled."

She tried to do the small talk when she really wanted to stop and kiss him. But she didn't know why he was here, and something told her she might not want to hear what he had to say.

"Nina. They found him."

She stopped walking. "They found him?"

He nodded slowly. "Last night."

"Where?" Her heart pounded out of her chest. She didn't know whether to be relieved or what.

The seriousness of his expression had her halting.

"He was in a motel just down the street. He had found you."

Her knees buckled and she dropped her coffee.

He tossed his cup on the ground and caught her. "Come on. Hang on to me. It's okay. I knew last night they had a lead but I didn't realize how close it was or that it would lead them right down the street. Or I would never have let you come home last night."

"How did he find me?"

"Well, against all odds, the morning show was partly to blame. Someone saw it and they were online and knew your work. They mentioned it reminded them of a painting they had of yours. He had an ongoing search for your name. And he got an alert. It was that simple. He's obviously obsessed, and you were right—he came for you. I don't want to scare you but he's being held and he had a lot of stuff with him. Things that will keep him behind bars for a long time."

He wrapped his arms around her and held her as she hung on to him.

She trembled from fear and relief at the same time. "He's not getting out?"

"Not if we have anything to do with it. But you'll be safe. Nina, I love you and I'm not going to let anything happen to you. If you don't mind, I'm going to stick to you like glue. I'd like to do it for the rest of your life, but it's probably too soon to mention that, so at least until we know he's not getting out."

"I'd like that. And Jackson, I mean forever…if you're serious."

She had found him and after what she'd been through, she wasn't going to let him go.

He smiled, looking into her eyes. "When this is finished, you can decide that. I rushed you."

She held onto him and knew she wasn't going to change her mind.

CHAPTER TWENTY-THREE

"**L**ook, that's Jackson and Nina on the beach." Lisa came out onto the edge of the veranda, peering out at the beach.

Alice had already spotted them. They'd been talking earnestly, him holding her in his arms. From this distance, she couldn't tell what they were talking about but her heart swelled seeing them together. "Yes, it's them." They were so cute together. Not just cute, but perfect.

"Has he kissed her?"

Alice grinned at her friend. "Not that I've seen. But they've been talking like that for a few moments. I wish I could see their expressions better. I think they are falling in love."

"I think they are and might just be realizing it," Lisa said. "Do you think you'll ever remarry?"

Alice looked at her friend. She sank down in the chair and set her coffee on the tabletop. "Right now, I can't think about something like that. But, you know, there's so many things to consider. For instance, I had such a wonderful marriage with William. Sure, like all marriages, it wasn't perfect. We had our problems—what couple doesn't? But in the overall aspect of marriages, it was wonderful. I loved him so much. What if I were to remarry and marry a terrible person, like your ex? Someone who tramples on my heart and leaves me for some younger woman, and then I have to deal with that emotional baggage like you're dealing with? No, I don't know. I'm not sure I'm that brave. Right now, I just need to open this inn and watch my boys find love—at least I hope they do."

"I hear you, sister. I am right there with you." Lisa held up her coffee mug. "Here's to finding ourselves on Star Gazer Island. In this inn. I feel good about it."

Alice, smiling, lifted her coffee cup and touched the edge of Lisa's mug. "To finding ourselves on Star Gazer Island. At Star Gazer Inn. Overlooking Corpus Christi Bay."

Lisa looked around. "Alice, this is what new

beginnings are made of. Friendship, and support, and having the courage to shoot for the stars and start over."

Alice smiled. "I think you're right."

CHAPTER TWENTY-FOUR

Time flew after the cattle sale and charity dinner. So much happened in the sale's aftermath. They learned that Nina had been hiding out from a scam artist who had not only stolen from her but had threatened her. And that he had followed her because of the television show featuring the inn and the small segment showing Nina's art. Alice and Lisa were in shock knowing that through Nina's art being recognized the stalker had come to town and tried to get to Nina. The knowledge that she had been responsible for bringing this person back into Nina's life after she had been hiding out for three years from the crazy man horrified Alice. And yet Nina, so sweet, had assured her that in the end this had been the best way because she couldn't continue to hide the rest of her life. And she had known the risk the day that she had chosen to sell paintings to Alice. Still, it did not settle well with Alice.

She had come to peace with it when Jackson told her she had thought she was helping Nina. And the fact that through it all Jackson and Nina had found each other. Alice had believed from the first moment she met Nina that she was perfect for her oldest son. And now they were dating exclusively, and if Alice were a betting woman, she would believe that soon there would be announcements of wedding plans. But she knew that Jackson wasn't one to just jump into things and after everything that Nina had been through, with her late husband and then this stalker, Alice was afraid Nina might have a hard time with commitment. And who could blame her?

Lisa, however, had pointed out that Nina would have never even considered a relationship with Jackson had she not already been certain he was nothing like the two horrible men who had been in her life recently. "Your Jackson is an amazing man," Lisa had said, standing there in the kitchen with her hands on her hips. "He's not like my horrible ex, Mason, and Nina's horrible examples of the male species—I refuse to call them even bad examples of men because I don't feel like they classify to be called men. But when I look at

Jackson, when I look at any of your sons, I recognize quality men and they get that from William leading by example. And your love and leadership as well."

Alice was so touched by her friend's words. "Thank you for that."

"No thanks needed, it is the truth. They're carrying on William's legacy of love, respect, kindness, and knowledge of how to treat a woman well. And I believe Nina has recognized that and when the time comes for Jackson to ask for her hand in marriage, I believe it will be a simple answer for Nina. Mark my words." Lisa had smiled broadly and then turned back to the counter and began preparing yet another experimental dish for the inn's menu.

Alice had to hope and believe that everything Lisa had been through that she understood how a jilted, mistreated woman would feel. And she prayed Lisa was right because she loved Nina and she would welcome Nina as her first daughter-in-law. So she was thinking positively and believing that they were meant to be. One great thing about it was that it had Jackson coming to town more often. And that pleased her.

Today Seth had finished the bathrooms, and they were gorgeous. They were so beautiful, so top of the line luxury, spa like bathrooms, she knew they would thrill her guests as they did her. She was glad that she had hired Seth to build the pavilion and he would start that on Monday. Truth be told, she wasn't ready for him to not be here. To not be around. She had grown fond of him and used to seeing him working around the inn. She had learned he was a quality caliber man. A man who, after five years, still carried flowers to his wife's grave. A kind and gentle man who seemed to understand where Alice was in her life, transitioning from a life with William to a life without William and now to a life where she was trying to move forward. But she was doing that with her focus on the inn. Everything else she was not rushing. Because it was hard and she wasn't to the point of thinking about dating someone and loving someone else seemed an impossible thought.

Lisa stated her opinion on that too, pausing icing a decadent chocolate truffle cake she pointed her spatula at Alice. "You don't have to marry the man, Alice. You just might need to consider going out on that boat with him. You told me he invited you to go out on the boat weeks ago. Just take a ride. Have a glass of wine, or a mimosa, or a simple glass of iced tea, lemonade, anything, but just go with him on the boat and enjoy yourself. And before you tell me you don't have time, I want you to tell me when was the last time you did something that had nothing to do with work? Because I know you love this inn, but everything about this inn has to do with your work. Go. Tell Seth you will ride with him on his boat for a sunset evening. I am confident he will not make a move on you. He respects you too much, you can see it in his eyes when he talks to you. The man understands exactly where you are because he's been there. You're not like me, you haven't been jilted, you haven't had your heart ripped out and trashed. No Alice, you've seen the best of a relationship, you've seen the beauty of a relationship. It was just taken away from you far too early. You just need to relax and have some fun. Go on a boat ride." And after her little tirade she gave her a smile, then went back to her cake.

Now standing here in the kitchen by herself on a Saturday morning, watching the waves roll in as she thought about picking up the phone and calling Seth, asking him if he was going out on his boat today. But she didn't need to call and ask him because she knew he would be on the boat. She knew that when he wasn't working, he spent a lot of his time on that boat. She wondered if it was because he was lonely. She was lonely. Oh, she had her kids and Nina and she had Lisa, but it just wasn't the same as it had been visiting with William. She missed him, their time together so much. She ached for him, for what they'd had, and when she was near Seth, she felt...so very close to having what she'd had with her William.

She didn't kid herself, there could never be

anything like what she'd had with her husband, and yet she found herself looking forward to seeing Seth each morning when he came to work. She enjoyed talking to him. Still, she couldn't pick up the phone and call him, she just couldn't do it.

Feeling restless, she chose instead to go to town. Walking over to the kitchen cabinet she picked up her small purse and strapped it over her body, picked up her wide-brimmed blue hat and placed it on her head and then perched her oversized, dark shades on her nose and she headed to town. Getting out would do her good. Monday would be busy as some new beds were being moved in and she would make final decorating decisions about each room. They had set a date for the opening of the inn and she had guests booked. It was exciting.

And yet as she walked, her thoughts went to Seth. It was disturbing. Guilt filled her that most of her day so far had been spent thinking about her contractor. William would be the first to tell her to move on, to go on a boat ride with the man. She could hear him as if speaking from the puffy white clouds in the perfectly sky-blue sky. "For Pete's sake, Alice, don't sit home and hibernate. Go on the boat ride. Move forward. I'm long gone, darlin', and I'm not coming back." Tears pricked her eyes.

Someone waved from across the street, one of the

ladies who worked at the grocery store. She waved back, blinking away the tears she sniffed and drew in a breath of strength and then she pushed the guilty feelings away. At least for now. William was right. He lingered in her thoughts, in her head these days, always pushing her to move on. It was sometimes aggravating. Maybe she didn't want to move on in that way.

When she reached the main section of shops, she was relieved because now she could go in and out of the shops and let her mind be busy searching for those perfect accessory items for the inn. Afterwards she would eat lunch at the pier and enjoy the atmosphere, enjoy watching the pelicans fly over the water, she loved watching how graceful the awkward birds were over the water. She'd soak up the sunshine. She'd be happy.

She would relax because Lisa was right, she did need to take time for herself. That could be the problem, she needed to start reaching out to her friends, start having lunch dates again. She and Lisa had had lunch a few times, but she was always too busy for more. She was going to have to fix that.

She bought a couple of items, a little plaque that said, "No hurry smell the breeze". And another that said, "Let the blue bird of joy fill you". The blue bird of joy. Her grandfather had always talked about the bluebird of happiness and the sign when she saw it reminded her of him. Even though he had passed away when she was a small girl she still remembered his happy smile and his jubilant laughter and joy.

She stood there in the middle of the store staring at the little sign and was determined to have that spirit. She'd picked it up and felt herself coming out of her melancholy state. She had just come out of a shop when a wind chime with sparkling pale blue glass caught her eye. Instead of watching where she was going, she was staring at the sparkling glass and she ran straight into someone. Hit them so hard her shades fell off her head where she'd perched them while shopping.

"Oh, I'm so sorry," she gasped as hands wrapped around her shoulders, steadying her and then she looked up into the startled pale blue eyes of Seth.

"Are you okay?" he asked, reaching down to retrieve her sunshades from the ground for her. He handed them to her. "You hit hard. I didn't hurt you, did I?"

She didn't have a voice at first because she had been thinking of him all morning and now here he was. "No. No, I'm fine. I'm sorry I wasn't paying attention. I'm shopping and I had my mind on something in the window." She didn't even know what she had been looking at now as all of her thoughts had flown away.

"Then I'm glad you're okay, but happy to run into

you."

She felt the same way but didn't say so.

They stepped out of the way so people could go into the shop. He looked different today wearing a T-shirt with an anchor on it and he wore casual cargo shorts and boat shoes, not jeans and work boots. "You look relaxed today," she said, smiling at him, feeling lighter-hearted than she had all day.

"Boat attire. I'm picking up my lunch and then heading out on the boat."

The boat. She thought about that boat and that ride and him. "It's a beautiful day to be on the boat. You should probably have a marvelous time."

"I'm hoping so." He stared at her for a long moment. "I know I asked you this awhile back, but it is a beautiful day and if you wanted to go, I'd sure welcome your company. I can pick up an extra order for lunch and we can eat on the boat and watch for dolphins and do a little fishing if you like fishing. If not, you could just sit back and relax, or read something on your phone if you have an app to read on."

She smiled, hearing the nervousness in his voice. He was hesitant about asking her, and he was very prepared for her to say no. Realizing this touched her and on a whim, she nodded.

And then she used her voice. "I would like that."

His brows knit, then slowly he smiled. "You're sure?"

"Yes. Yes, Seth, I'm very serious. I would like very much to go on a boat ride with you."

And just like that, she had taken another step forward.

* * *

Seth had been stunned when Alice accepted his invitation to join him on his boat. He hadn't offered again since that first time when they had been at the inn looking at the bathroom in the upper story. He had gotten the message loud and clear that she wasn't ready, not only not to date, but she wasn't ready to even form a friendship with a man. It had only been sixteen months since she'd lost her husband; he added the time he'd known her and realized it was now getting closer to eighteen months since her husband, William, had died in a tragic accident. For him it had been a long five years. Five years of trying to adjust to life without his Jen and finding anyone who even remotely interested him to ask out. Alice was the first woman to stir his interest in all that time. He didn't hold anything against her for refusing his invitation to go on a boat ride. He completely understood. But he had been disappointed. Now, after they had picked up their lunches and were walking down the pier to the marina toward his boat, he was determined not to screw this up. She had agreed to go out on his boat nothing more and the stakes were high, and if he messed up, he knew she wouldn't go on a boat ride or anything else with him maybe forever.

This was his one shot, and it had him torn up inside. Him a fifty-nine-year-old man, and he was more nervous than he had been all those years ago when he'd asked Jennifer on their first date.

"So which one is your boat?" Alice asked, looking up at him, her beautiful face sending that now familiar tremor of joy through him. Joy he hadn't known in forever. It was unusual just to feel joy looking at someone, but that's the feeling that had settled over him ever since he had started working for Alice renovating the inn for her. And he had been content just feeling that every day when he had gone to work. They had worked quietly in the house together, passing each other in the hallway, her bringing him food to test, being Lisa's food tester was a job perk he also enjoyed. Because Lisa Blair was a master with food. But it was Alice that made this job mean more to him than any renovating job he'd ever had. He had been very grateful when Alice had asked him if he would build a pavilion for her in the backyard of the inn. The project lengthened his stay and his time to be around her. And he thanked God every morning that Monday morning he was going back to work at the inn. This boat ride was a bonus trip, and again he couldn't screw it up.

"Which boat is yours?" she asked again as they walked down the pier.

"It's the pale blue one there on the right-hand side. It's a twenty-seven foot fishing boat, not too big and not too little. It has two engines, so no worries if one goes out we can always get back to shore, and it's an unsinkable vessel so if anything were to happen and we started taking on water it wouldn't sink so you don't need to worry about that either. I'm just tootling around the island here and hoping to see some dolphins today, just getting out of the house. Might go over and stop off at a refuge see some birds if I got the hankering. So we can do whatever you want to do today. And here we are." He stopped at the boat. "Hold on and let me put this food away." He stepped onto the side of the boat and then onto the step inside the boat. The boat swayed but he was so used to the feeling he barely felt it as he set the food in his captain's chair.

Then he turned back and held his hand out to her. She slipped her small hand into his and his heart kicked up like he'd just run around the world and back. She stepped onto the side of the boat and not wanting her to fall, he grabbed her around the waist and lifted her into the boat. It felt right holding her. Like that day on the stairs when she had almost fallen and he had grabbed her, snatching her to him to protect her from tumbling down the stairs. She was small and nowhere near anything like his, Jen, but she had felt right there in his arms. She had quickly gotten a hold of herself and moved out of his arms, and he had regretted every day he had not gotten to hold her longer. But today he let her go quickly, not wanting to mess up this opportunity. Today the only thing he was focused on was helping her relax around him and letting her enjoy this day. Letting her know that in him she had a friend.

And if that was all it ever was between them, he would be okay with that.

Not really, but he would be. She looked up at him, not smiling but looking confused, probably on what her next step was.

"If you want to sit there in the chair right there, I'll be sitting in the other one driving. He picked up the bags of food and placed them in the ice chest behind his seat to keep the sandwiches cool.

She sat down. "It's a lovely boat. It's perfect. Actually, it's not one of those that you have to sit high up, and it's not cumbersome with a big cabin below or anything like that. I'm sure you have a lot of good days here on this boat."

"I do. I had a smaller boat. Before Jen died. I

didn't really see any need to have a bigger boat before that because with my job, not this job but my job at a Fortune 500 company I had worked for, I worked long, long hours and we didn't get down to the boat that often. But as soon as I knew I wasn't going back to that job but instead was opening my contracting business, I got this boat."

"It matches your eyes."

He was startled that she made that connection. "Yeah, I didn't really think about it when I bought the boat but a friend of mine brought that to my attention. I just like the look of these blue boats on the water. It's a color that makes me happy."

She held his gaze. "The blue boat of joy or happiness." She smiled.

"What?"

Her smile broadened. "The bluebird of happiness is an old saying, but my grandfather used to say the bluebird of joy. I just changed it because this boat represents that to you."

"True, it fits."

"Blue. Like the water and the sky there's something about a blue sky, even when storms come you always know it's going to pass and the sky is going to turn blue again. It's hopeful." She looked away at the sky, and he thought he heard some emotion in her words.

She was right. "Exactly. I think we're ready, so sit there and I'll push us off and we'll head out to where the sky meets the water. We're on the hunt for dolphin, well, porpoise, better call it the right name because I fish for dolphin, mahi-mahi. Porpoise and dolphin aren't the same thing but some people get alarmed when I tell them I caught a bunch of dolphins for dinner."

She smiled. "I actually know the difference in a dolphin and a porpoise. And I think if I were fishing, I would be fishing for mahi-mahi also. I love to eat it."

"Then we have that in common. I can fix an excellent mahi dish. I might even have to teach Lisa how to fix it. It's that good."

"If it's that good," she said. "You're going to have to fix it for me sometime."

"It's that good," he said, as he untied the boat from the pier, and after taking his seat he smiled at her. He looked at her realizing that that was somewhat of an invitation, she looked as startled as he was at her words.

"I mean for Lisa and I," she clarified.

"I can do that. I need to repay you two ladies for all the excellent food that you've provided for me."

She smiled and relaxed. And he breathed a sigh of relief, worrying that she had seen his expression and thought he would insist or have been asking her on a date and she accepted.

"Are you ready?"

"I'm ready."

He pulled back the throttle and the boat sped up heading forward out into the bay. And as the salty wind blew across his face, and the sun shined down on him, it was the first time he had driven in this boat that he felt actual peace. Oh, he was still nervous, but he was happy. Totally happy. And hopeful.

They found the porpoise, sleek, gray, playful, and perfect. Alice loved the boat ride, and as Seth eased the boat along while she watched the show the porpoise put on for them, she knew she smiled more in those moments than she had in a long, long time. It felt so very good.

She thought of her William in those moments, watching as the porpoise displayed their acrobatic skills, dancing on the water, twisting and turning in the air and diving back into the blue water leaving rippling marks where they'd disappeared, only to rise up once more to start a new show. Why had William ridden his horse into that river, knowing the danger? Why had he taken the risk? It was something she might never know. She wanted to call him back. Rewind their life before that moment but she couldn't. She closed her eyes and let the tightness around her heart case.

Deciding to put all her efforts into a new

beginning, getting the Star Gazer Inn open for business had been a decision she'd been compelled to do. It had been a great decision and felt so right. Her renewed friendship with Lisa and her new friendship with Nina made everything worthwhile already, and she could only look forward to the days ahead as they opened the inn and as Nina and Jackson started their life together. Hopefully that would progress quickly.

But Seth had been a surprise. Meeting him was not something she'd anticipated. And yet she knew he would be a part of her future. How much a part, she wasn't yet certain, but she felt happy and there was the promise of…more. As if like the porpoise diving into the sea and leaving the ripples of a beautiful life and then emerging once more to start all over again, it was exciting. She had taken a step forward, even though she felt nervous about even considering more than friendship with Seth. She was stronger these days and beginning to feel more and more like the woman she'd been before tragedy had taken William. Could she ever let her heart risk that kind of pain again? That deep ripping away of her heart?

She took a halting breath.

"Are you okay?" Seth asked. His deep voice full of concern.

She must have been so deeply lost in thought that her expression showed the pain of those thoughts. She looked at Seth and decided to be honest. "I'm feeling confused, and the pain of losing William hit me hard just now."

"I'm sorry. We can go back?"

She gave him a soft smile. "No, we can't go back. Hear me out, I'm feeling the pain because I know it's time to push forward and that's why I'm here now, with you. I think going forward won't be easy. Did you feel that?"

He nodded and slowed the boat to a stop. Then turned his chair to face her.

"I did. But I moved slowly. You are the first woman I've felt strongly about pursuing. I'm not saying that to scare you or run you away, I'm just being honest. I think we are mature adults and honesty is the only way to go into this. You may have days when you feel you've moved forward and then days you feel yourself move back into the safe zone. I'm here to tell you I understand and will support you on how you want this relationship to go. You are in control."

Well, it was honest, and she needed that. "Then I'll tell you what I feel. I am drawn to you. I feel a connection to you that I've never felt before I met William and have never felt after falling for William. So now you know. But I'm not sure I can ever love again. Or let myself love again. You know how painful it is to lose."

He smiled and leaned forward and gently took her hands in his. His touch was warm and comforting, and more…it sent her heart thundering at the simple touch.

"Alice, I never thought I could think about loving again. Or dating again. Or risking my heart again. But I'm learning that I'd never have chosen to go through life without loving Jen, even if I'd known she was going to die before me. Life is made better by having known her and loved her. And you feel the same way about William. Right?"

She nodded, feeling tears.

"I've had longer to realize I want to feel that love, that connection with someone else. My heart is big enough to love again. I can't explain it. I'd never believed it. But it's so. Maybe if I was older, I wouldn't feel this way. I want to be your friend. Your good friend. I want to see where we can go from here, but at your pace. And only you can decide if you want more. So, for now, let me be your friend. Let me be the person you take boat rides with and watch the sunset with when you feel like sharing those things."

She stared into his blue eyes, and the tension that had taken hold of her eased. She trusted Seth. She smiled. "I'd like that very much."

And she knew it was true.

Seth smiled and stood, and as the boat gently

rocked, he pulled her to a standing position and wrapped his arms around her. "Thank you. I just wanted to give you a hug and tell you I'm here for you, Alice. But you know, you're doing great on your own. I'm just enjoying watching you."

She looked up at him, enjoying being in his arms again. "I'm thinking this is all a part of what new beginnings are made of, the courage to take a step out of my comfort zone, excitement at seeing accomplishment and satisfaction at knowing even if it's hard at times, I'm pushing onward."

His smile widened. "I believe you're right." He released her and turned her so she was looking back across the water in the distance to where the inn could be seen along the shore. "You've brought that inn back to life, it's resilient like you. You will be all right, Alice."

She stared at the inn, her inn, and knew that she was resilient too. And she was going to be alright.

"Yes, I am," she said, looking at Seth. And then she smiled because she knew it was true.

Dear Readers,

Thank you so much for reading! I hope you enjoyed this book and that you'll follow Alice and Seth's journey into the next book. Get your copy of WHAT DREAMS ARE MADE OF today.

WHAT DREAMS ARE MADE OF
Star Gazer Inn of Corpus Christi Bay, Book Two

New beginnings take determination…

Welcome back to Star Gazer Inn. Alice McIntyre's fresh start after buying the Star Gazer Inn is filling her days, and she's now ready to open with the help of her best friend Lisa's culinary skills and uplifting attitude. And her soon-to-be daughter-in-law Nina by her side, too.

And the magic of her new friend and contractor Seth Roark's tireless attention to detail.

Seth and Alice have both suffered loss, both are starting over, and both are treating this new friendship and attraction they feel toward each other with caution.

Alice's son Dallas is realizing he may not have what it takes to continue riding in the pro rodeo bull riding circuit. He's home at the South Texas McIntyre Ranch after injuring his shoulder and checking out what's going on at his mother's new inn. When he meets a beautiful woman on the beach under unusual circumstances, he has no idea how his life is about to change…

Meanwhile:
Riley McIntyre is full speed ahead on getting the new "glamping" venue on the ranch's coastal beachfront property up and going for the ladies who like a little glamor and luxury to their camping experience.

Jackson and Nina are planning their wedding.

Lisa's past is causing problems and with the opening of the inn, Alice needs her to be focused and her culinary skills to be at their best. Can she handle the pressure?

Three women find friendship and courage on the shores of Corpus Christi Bay. Come visit the Star Gazer Inn, with a side trip to the McIntyre Ranch, as Alice finds her way between two worlds.

This new series follows Alice, her sons, and her friends—and new loves—on the South Texas coast with its sparkling topaz water.

You'll want to dip your toes in and stay awhile.

More Books by Debra Clopton

Star Gazer Inn of Corpus Christi Bay
What New Beginnings are Made of (Book 1)
What Dreams are Made of (Book 2)
What Hopes are Made of (Book 3)

Sunset Bay Romance
Longing for Forever (Book 1)
Longing for a Hero (Book 2)
Longing for Love (Book 3)
Longing for Ever After (Book 4)
Longing for You (Book 5)
Longing for Us (Book 6)

Texas Brides & Bachelors
Heart of a Cowboy (Book 1)
Trust of a Cowboy (Book 2)
True Love of a Cowboy (Book 3)

New Horizon Ranch Series
Her Texas Cowboy: Cliff (Book 1)
Rescued by Her Cowboy: Rafe (Book 2)
Protected by Her Cowboy: Chase (Book 3)
Loving Her Best Friend Cowboy: Ty (Book 4)

Family for a Cowboy: Dalton (Book 5)
The Mission of Her Cowboy: Treb (Book 6)
Maddie's Secret Baby (Book 7)
This Cowgirl Loves This Cowboy: Austin (Book 8)

Turner Creek Ranch Series
Treasure Me, Cowboy (Book 1)
Rescue Me, Cowboy (Book 2)
Complete Me, Cowboy (Book 3)
Sweet Talk Me, Cowboy (Book 4)

Cowboys of Ransom Creek
Her Cowboy Hero (Book 1)
The Cowboy's Bride for Hire (Book 2)
Cooper: Charmed by the Cowboy (Book 3)
Shane: The Cowboy's Junk-Store Princess (Book 4)
Vance: Her Second-Chance Cowboy (Book 5)
Drake: The Cowboy and Maisy Love (Book 6)
Brice: Not Quite Looking for a Family (Book 7)

Texas Matchmaker Series
Dream With Me, Cowboy (Book 1)
Be My Love, Cowboy (Book 2)
This Heart's Yours, Cowboy (Book 3)
Hold Me, Cowboy (Book 4)
Be Mine, Cowboy (Book 5)
Operation: Married by Christmas (Book 6)

Cherish Me, Cowboy (Book 7)
Surprise Me, Cowboy (Book 8)
Serenade Me, Cowboy (Book 9)
Return To Me, Cowboy (Book 10)
Love Me, Cowboy (Book 11)
Ride With Me, Cowboy (Book 12)
Dance With Me, Cowboy (Book 13)

Windswept Bay Series
From This Moment On (Book 1)
Somewhere With You (Book 2)
With This Kiss (Book 3)
Forever and For Always (Book 4)
Holding Out For Love (Book 5)
With This Ring (Book 6)
With This Promise (Book 7)
With This Pledge (Book 8)
With This Wish (Book 9)
With This Forever (Book 10)
With This Vow (Book 11)

About the Author

Bestselling author Debra Clopton has sold over 2.5 million books. Her book OPERATION: MARRIED BY CHRISTMAS has been optioned for an ABC Family Movie. Debra is known for her contemporary, western romances, Texas cowboys and feisty heroines. Sweet romance and humor are always intertwined to make readers smile. A sixth generation Texan she lives with her husband on a ranch deep in the heart of Texas. She loves being contacted by readers.

Visit Debra's website at www.debraclopton.com

Sign up for Debra's newsletter at
www.debraclopton.com/contest/

Check out her Facebook at
www.facebook.com/debra.clopton.5

Follow her on Twitter at @debraclopton

Contact her at debraclopton@ymail.com

If you enjoyed reading *What New Beginnings are Made of*, I would appreciate it if you would help others enjoy this book, too.

Recommend it. Please help other readers find this book by recommending it to friends, reader's groups and discussion boards.

Review it. Please tell other readers why you liked this book by reviewing it on the retail site you purchased it from or Goodreads. If you do write a review, please send an email to debraclopton@ymail.com so I can thank you with a personal email. Or visit me at: www.debraclopton.com.

Made in United States
North Haven, CT
08 November 2021

10939952R00167